About the Author

Kari Utoslahti has worked for decades as a journalist in Oulu, Finland. First in a newspaper called *Kaleva* and after that in a local paper *Forum24*. He took his bachelor degree at Oulu University in 1994. Now his pen flies in the world of fiction. At present he lives in Vantaa with his spouse Tiina. He is also a grandpa to four grandchildren.

Papparazzing in London

Kari Utoslahti

Papparazzing in London

Olympia Publishers
London

www.olympiapublishers.com
OLYMPIA PAPERBACK EDITION

Copyright © Kari Utoslahti 2023

The right of Kari Utoslahti to be identified as author of
this work has been asserted in accordance with sections 77 and 78 of
the Copyright, Designs and Patents Act 1988.

All Rights Reserved

No reproduction, copy or transmission of this publication
may be made without written permission.
No paragraph of this publication may be reproduced,
copied or transmitted save with the written permission of the publisher,
or in accordance with the provisions
of the Copyright Act 1956 (as amended).

Any person who commits any unauthorised act in relation to
this publication may be liable to criminal
prosecution and civil claims for damage.

A CIP catalogue record for this title is
available from the British Library.

ISBN: 978-1-80074-984-9

This is a work of fiction.
Names, characters, places and incidents originate from the writer's
imagination. Any resemblance to actual persons, living or dead, is
purely coincidental.

First Published in 2023

Olympia Publishers
Tallis House
2 Tallis Street
London
EC4Y 0AB

Printed in Great Britain

Dedication

I dedicate this book to my wife, Tiina.

INVITATION TO LONDON

Papparazzi, the proverbial photographer, had struck gold with his Banksy In Helsinki photo expo. The success was so great that after it was over, Graham Stone, the editor in chief of *London Star*, had offered employment in the tabloid to the Finn. A rental studio for employee housing was included in the fixed-term contract. The small attic room of a traditional house accommodated a lounge, bedroom, kitchenette and a ridiculously small bathroom. Papparazzi had also kept his home in Finland as an insurance policy. The shooter was provided with a brand-new Ford Fiesta at this point. Despite his concerns on driving on the left-hand side no collisions had taken place so far. He was mastering his driving on a daily basis.

The shoots of Banksy's creations had made a great impact on Graham Stone. The penman had visited The Snow White Gallery in Piccadilly Arcade frequently. The contract had been signed and sealed on the spot. He had reasoned his recruitment with wanting to get a new buzz, blood and a power boost to the illustrations for the newspaper he was leading. In addition to shooting in the bushes, he took pictures in the press releases and prearranged gigs. *London Star* was a part of a larger The Ace Media Group involving Papparazzi with shootings as required to other parties. The work provided more stability but a bit less freedom.

Rob Lane, a deliveryman and jack-of-all-trades on the media company, helped Papparazzi whenever he had time from his other jobs. He had a background in racing, which gave him an advantage in shuttling among the jammed traffic of the metropole. The most distinctive feature of his character was self-mockery. He never lost his humorous insight even when the going went rough.

During the buzz of the Banksy expo he was also bonding with Edna White, the gallerist of The Snow White Gallery. Her relationship with Mandi, the practical rotator of the Papparazzi Gallery in Helsinki, was also close. The galleries would stay in close contact in the future as well. The British lady had a very snazzy, individual and freshly different style. She was wearing specs from the Twiggy collection. On her most recent visit to London Mandi had revealed a secret concerning Edna to Papparazzi.

"Edna is a nympho. Look out for yourself!"

Mandi had admitted missing the co-owner of the gallery she was managing. Especially with hanging and choosing the pictures on the forthcoming expos she was lacking advice from her more experienced co-owner. Thanks to the digital connections they were able to exchange information. There were also other people missing him in Finland. His accomplice the Machine, his grown-up daughter Julia with her family and his latest better half, the photographer Mammarazzi, with whom he had mutually agreed to separate. His former wife Raisa was more than happy having more distance between them. Her sex life was flourishing as she was having the most wonderful toy boy keeping her bed warm.

Papparazzi's repatriation to London had not been a rosy walk in the park. In a newspaper interview George Bamby, the most famous paparazzo in London, had sworn to give him a good run for his money. In the end of the story, he reached the final climax.

"I'm gonna fix that scarfy clown's ass!"

BOND ON THE RUN

Papparazzi was setting a drone with Rob in front of the Lexham Gardens. According to a hot tip they had received, Daniel Craig aka James Bond was spending a light-hearted summer night in a private garden in there. The Duo Ramshackle of London wondered why no other snappers were on the spot. Chances of getting once-in-a-lifetime photos brought more edge to their mission. Before long a camera-drone darted to snoop around the vicinity. Rob steered the miniature aircraft expertly – he had taught Papparazzi to handle it as well. The crowd gathered under the cherry trees was easy to detect. As they couldn't single out the actor of Agent 007, they had no choice but to keep the device up in the air keeping it inconspicuous.

"In the States a few celebs have done some target practice on the drones hovering on their grounds with their shot-guns," Papparazzi stated, browsing the settings of his SRL camera.

"Don't worry about that in here, although there will probably be a crack shot like James Bond present in the facilities," Rob assured while keeping his eyes on the controls of the drone and his smartphone where he could see the images from the quadcopter.

"If he enjoys being in there and we can get some footage of him, this will be one of my most unforgettable gigs."

"Definitely, Boss!"

They kept their eyes on their watches anxiously under the glow of the setting sun. Time progressed with squat. The passersby let the duo get on with their business in peace. In their eyes those two were just a couple of overaged youtubers.

Suddenly Rob gave a thumbs up and Papparazzi joined in. Daniel Craig strutted in the garden holding a champagne glass in his hand! Rob locked the device on the target. The star got plenty of taps on his shoulders. Probably they were praising his heroic performance in the film *No Time To Die*. He didn't even take an accidental peek upwards, all they could see was his hair and suit. As the battery was almost dead, Rob grounded the drone back to the starting point. The lack of facial images was a mood killer. Obviously their tactics had proven to be too cautious. While Rob was changing the battery, a new and braver strategy brightened for both of them. The second time around they would be bolder, landing the gadget on the level of the Bond's upper body.

"Then just bluntly shoot straight on his face."

As excellent as their plan seemed on paper, it proved to fall short in a jiffy. Daniel Craig's frolicking time was up. He dashed past them towards his sporty style Aston Martin, parked wrongly on two parking spots. It was his way of sparing his car from getting scratched. A glance from the cameramen was a sign of registration of them and their intentions. The frown on his face made it clear how much he disliked them. It took him less than a second to vanish deep inside his scarlet Roadrunner. Caught with their pants down, Duo Ramshackle rushed into action. They squeezed inside the olive-green BMW X6 with their bags and baggage. They burned rubber on the chase for James Bond. The engines roared and powers increased. Although the vehicles skidded in the corners, both drivers controlled their cars perfectly. As Bond zigzagged past the slower rides, the Beamer stuck like a glue behind it. Papparazzi admired Rob's driving skills.

"You are quite a roadrunner, aren't you? Bond would have lost me completely by now."

"He's not giving up easy on us! But this isn't my first rodeo either."

A mother of all slowpokes emerged in front of 007. The secret agent honked impatiently trying to get the front driver to move over. Once it had no effect on the driver, short-tempered Bond begun pushing the vehicle with increasing speed. Separation occurred, when Bond took a tight turn on the left and the Citroen 2CV swayed its way into the nearby lamppost. After his sudden stop, a heated-up face of an old geezer emerged from the open window. The man had a strong resemblance to Richard Bucket from the TV series *Keeping Up Appearances*.

In no time the vortex of Cromwell Road swallowed the speed maniacs in the direction of Westminster. The gas pedals were stepped on – they slowed down with screeching brakes only when passing a traffic camera. Rob knew the time had come to act and boldly pushed the BMW right beside the Aston Martin. Icy stares met. Once Papparazzi pushed the shutter release, he realised that instead of a top shoot of an agent all he got was a miss. Bond had once again taken the lead at a lightning speed. The gasoline in Rob's blood was mixed with a healthy dose of adrenalin. His senses and grips sharpened even more. Close passing followed one another in quick succession. Other drivers honked with irritation letting the green and red devils pass them as they did to emergency vehicles. At the same time Papparazzi noticed two cars colliding their sidemirrors near the Natural History Museum. They came crumpling down hanging from the wires like Cocker spaniel's ears. It was an outright miracle that no more metal had crashed during the chase. And there were not a single police officer in sight.

The name of the road changed into Brompton Road and Rob gestured the camera guy to look on the right.

"Harrods!"

"Do you want to go shopping before we continue our chase?"

"We don't have the time, I think…"

After passing Hyde Park Corner underground station, Bond and Rob took a brisk pace cutting the corners.

The momentous occasion occurred by the statue of Winston Churchill, when a VW Kleinbus favoured by the hippies emerged out of thin air from the Parliament Street. The red missile slipped it from the right and the green one from the left. They avoided contact by centimetres. The Westminster Bridge crossing over the River Thames was so packed with cars that their rushing hit the wall. They crawled forward in the middle of the convoy. There were a few cars between Duo Ramshackle and Craig giving him a chance to monitor his stalkers through his rear-view mirror.

"I have been waiting the whole time, if Bond will do his magic in the spirit of Quartermaster Q, that his car blasts some backfire towards us or it starts to bounce like a rubber-ball over the vehicles in front of him," Papparazzi stated.

Rob chuckled.

"In both cases our little adventure would be shut down there and then. It seems that the car fleeing in front of us is not a heavily armoured one equipped by Q."

"Then nothing will stop us!"

"Only this evening rush hour."

Papparazzi had a clear view of the nearby London Eye glowing in the rays of sun. One of the carriages flickered extraordinarily brightly in their direction.

"The Ferris wheel is blinking at us."

"Sparks have been flying in here before this. The bad guy Blofeld crashed on this bridge in *Spectre*. Bond could have finished him off but spared his life instead."

Papparazzi remembered the scene clearly as well.

"The movie made this place legendary. And now we are chasing Craig in here!"

"This is a once in a lifetime experience so we'd better enjoy every minute of it."

The jam showed signs of unravelling. Rob and Bond filled the gaps with their vehicles efficiently stepping on their accelerators with heavy feet. Their fellow drivers didn't have sufficient understanding of their efforts, waving their fists up to the daredevils.

Actual hullabaloo broke in the surroundings of Waterloo station. Turns and braking after another took place, once in a while they sped on the one-way streets in the wrong direction. The expressions on the faces of the on-comers were worth seeing, but both the violators of the traffic rules were able to dodge them skilfully. White and red-bricked apartment buildings, traffic signs, billboards and other road users scuttled before Papparazzi's eyes. He had no idea where they were burning rubber this time.

"Bond has everything at stake now. He has set his mind up to get rid of us!" Rob cried.

The tail lights of the Aston Martin loomed increasingly distantly. From time to time they vanished altogether and Rob was forced to draw straws on 007's route choices. The local knowledge of the deliveryman helped them to keep on the right track.

The batty chase of almost half an hour on the South Bank

took a sudden stop, when they turned on the Belvedere Road. All of a sudden, the secret agent parked his car in front of Brasserie Blanc and Pizza Express. He bounced out and ran away. As Rob was parking his vehicle behind the Aston Martin DBS Superleggera, Craig was taking a turn to the right leaping over a concrete barrier and ascending the stairs of the Southbank Centre. Whereafter Papparazzi grabbed his camera and Rob took his drone, they dashed after the fugitive. They run through the terrace square, turned right and saw the yellow-painted stairs they used for descending down to the bank of the River Thames. Upon arrival at the National Theatre the duo stood still in order to take a peek at their surroundings. The Queen's Walk was guarded by bushy plane trees and decorative lampposts. Lovers walked hand in hand and joggers flashed past. Rob noticed that the London Pride statue behind the stylised stone ring appeared to be a little off. On the top of the statue presenting two women was a man doing push-ups standing on his arms, his hands placed on top of the figurines' heads. The only person he could have been was the film star waiting for them! That's where they were going. As Papparazzi was raising his camera, the superstar somersaulted down through the air. He softened his landing with a forward roll. Craig headed straight towards poking them aside. Soon the shooters were on his heels. Their steps echoed against the tiling as they frolicked under the Waterloo Bridge. Occasionally Bond did cartwheels dirtying his suit in the process. Next came a jump high in the air and grabbing with both hands on the massive branch of a plane tree swinging himself to the next tree accompanied with a Tarzan-like howling. The next glide fell short so his scuttle went on once again on the solid ground.

"Can you snap any photos?"

"Certainly not! We're going so fast it's hard to keep up!"

"We really have to add fuel to the fire!"

The agent pushed through the gate to the Festival Pier. The crowd in front of the place had to clear the way for his followers. Going down on the pipe they heard the roar of a motorboat starting. It sounded like a rage ride. Upon arrival on the pier, they saw 007 ploughing his boat along the Thames. The boat's bow pointed east. They had faced the winner, shaken and stirred. Or had they? A snappy-dressed middle-aged gentleman was enjoying his packed lunch on his moored boat. He greeted Rob and Papparazzi by lifting his flat cap.

"He was in a hurry, that one! He downright flew into his boat. I have never seen anyone loosening the ropes and taking off so quickly. Really efficient operation."

The Duo Ramshackle confided him with their mission. The name Daniel Craig caught brought sparks to his eyes.

"I thought there was something vaguely familiar, but his chunky look made me deny the mere possibility him being the secret servant of Her Majesty."

"Well, that's the one and only!"

Would his streamlined luxury boat be available in order to continue the chase? He almost choked on a piece of bread when hearing their request. Once he had cleared his throat, he sounded hesitant.

"My picnic is barely in progress. I have been browsing the river scenery for more than an hour and had planned to have my lunch and ventilate my thoughts at this point. So, I won't be taking you up on your offer... Although Bond ignites me too!"

"This is an opportunity of a lifetime and the monetary compensation will be worth your while. Is two hundred pounds enough for your efforts?"

The gentleman shook his head as a sign of the answer being

no. Five hundred pounds made him take the bait. Related to the sealed deal he introduced himself in the spirit of Bond:

"My name is Nelson, Kevin Nelson!"

The boat named Ol' River was cast off in record time and it shot off with a full throttle. Kevin was rotating the rudder with whitened fingers. Papparazzi and Rob sat right behind him. Since it was already twilight time, the drone would be, in the foreseeable future, the only gadget enabling them to catch the shots they needed. At this point Bond was hopelessly far from them. On top of everything it felt like that the distance was growing constantly. According to Kevin, Bond had also significantly more water-horsepower in his boat.

Approaching the Tower Bridge, something unexpected occurred. The powerboat slowed down. Kevin assumed the gas was running low, or even running out altogether on Bond's boat.

"We might still be able to hit our target!"

As the gap was closing, Rob went through all the settings of his drone. The boat would be inside its range soon enough. They saw Bond dropping his anchor making their faces light with joy. The prey was within their reach! Papparazzi could also get some close-ups as well! The trackers' joy was premature due to 007 having one more ace up in his sleeve. He snapped the harness on and an ejector seat catapulted him up in the sky. When the parachute ballooned over his head Bond said:

"Hey, I'm flying!"

Doing so he dropped Papparazzi away from the shooting game. Rob instead was on fire letting his drone up in the air. The quadcopter got the target as Bond was descending on his parachute featuring the Union Jack on the bridge. They got a lot of pictures in different angles. The drone caught also how Bond took off his harness beside a beggar. The agent slipped a note into his dipper and wished him good night walking away. Although 'Skyfall' was playing as his earworm, the sky hadn't fallen on top of him. At least he had given those bush-shooters a good run for their money.

Under the bridge, stalkers were browsing the shots high-fiving each other. Especially the facials made a huge impact on them. *London Star* would get an exclusive scoop on this! In the wake of it the newest Bond pictures would be seen all over the global media. Papparazzi's inner account book showed that all the debts would transfer into receivables in gigantic scale making a good profit to his helpers as well. They decided to celebrate their accomplishment in the traditional British way at a local pub treating themselves with fish and chips and a cold beer. The Duo Ramshackle had truly deserved it.

HOT HIPS

Papparazzi was waiting for Edna to arrive at the platform of the Piccadilly Circus station. There was going to be an expo of contemporary art in Jo's Art Gallery in Marylebone opening soon, and they had asked Edna to prescreen it just to make sure that everything was in order. She had lured the Finnish photographer to join her. At the destination they were going to get to see visual artist Lesley Drury's art work before others. The painter was well known for her bold imagery. In her works she examined the basic questions of life such as sex, birth and death.

Edna popped up out of thin air in her body-hugging low-cut frock. Her auburn hair curled on her neck and ears. The jewellery and high heels complemented her eye-catching attire. Papparazzi was like melted wax in front of his lady in blue. They hugged lightly. His outfit choice in the sweaty heat was a blazer, striped T-shirt, light jeans and sneakers. As a cherry on top was his trade mark, a sailor-style scarf tied around his neck. Despite this he felt naked having left his camera bag at home by request of Edna. Usually it was always with him. The gallerist had convinced the linen head that his shooting gear was not needed this time.

The Bakerloo Line train stopped and they got on board. The timeworn carriage was as congested as the platform had been. It took them a while to get to sit side by side. They went through their past relations briefly. Papparazzi told her he had been divorced for quite some time now. The thing about his and Raisa's bundle of joy, Julia, living in Vantaa with her family was also settled. Papparazzi then focused on Edna's tale of her past. The deer-eyed Londoner had had her fair share of shorter and longer relationships, but she had never worn an engagement ring on her finger. She had no children.

"I have never hit it with Mr Right. Maybe it's not meant to be…"

"Before all one has to make sure it's the right one. On that basis you might one of these days find the counterpart and orange blossom of your life."

"Well, that is so sweet!"

Papparazzi's cheeks blushed. It was time to change the subject into a more professional one.

"For how long you have had your Snow White Gallery?"

"More than a decade now. I worked for other gallerists prior to that. The will of going for and implementing my own dreams speeded me up into the heart of London. My desire was to offer exhibition space to photographers – even to paparazzi."

"That is something we never had too much of. That's why I established Gallery Papparazzi in Helsinki. Now I am the silent partner in it. Magazine photographing is the thing for me, so that is my first priority."

"Mandi being such a busy businesswoman, you have nothing to worry about. She takes care of the practicalities in there. You can focus on gathering the proceeds in that part."

Papparazzi knew it all too well. But he also knew how so seemingly easy business could prove to be extremely hard on you.

"How much time even one expo takes with painting hangings, removals and moving. In addition comes the advertising, logistics and opening arrangements. The gallerist has to be present throughout the whole hullabaloo. Quite often the artists need the gallerist's shoulders to press their heads on for comfort and support in their creative distress," Edna accompanied.

"Nothing on that list is enough if no-one is buying those creations. You have to keep up the pace all the time," Papparazzi followed her lead.

The commodities differed from for example of car dealership radically. People were ready to pay tens of thousands of pounds for a car, but when it came to purchasing a painting the cost should have been between a few hundred and not more than a few thousand pounds. In the UK the gallerists collaborated more than for instance in the USA. On the island they understood the meaning of cooperation. In this delicate line of business, it made them stronger.

"In my own experience I can tell that I wouldn't have survived without this kind of safety net. Jo Demmen, the owner of Jo's Art Gallery, is one of my long-lasting partners. We do watch each other's backs and business as well."

Going through all of this made them smile. Needless to say, their work was the best in the world. Once they popped out of the depths of the Edgeware Road station into the landscape surrounded by skyscrapers, Papparazzi stole Edna's hand. She clenched it, and didn't let go. Their gazes also met. In Marylebone, in the Universe, was no-one else but them. Walking on the Bell Street, Papparazzi pondered how had this come about. They had been more involved in setting up his Banksy exhibition, at the opening and for some time afterwards but since then just occasionally. There had always been a strong connection between them. Chemistry had always been clicking well. Now every cell of his body urged to belong to this woman walking beside him.

After a short walk, they turned left. Behind the corner there was a high redbrick building holding Jo's Art Gallery's big solid glass wall at street level. The number of the sloping-roofed building was inserted in the wall with glass tiles. Papparazzi and Edna had barely broken their grip, as Joan and Lesley greeted them on the gallery door. The couple wore similar clothes glowing in rainbow colours. Jo dropped the keys of her namesake gallery on to Edna's hand and briefed:

"Take all the time you need on your grand tour around the expo like studio critics. If you have any suggestions for the last touches, write them down and leave the notes on my bureau. We are going for a drink together. Don't expect us to be coming back tonight."

"And I would love to hear your opinion on my expo!" Lesley added.

The plot was set. Edna and Papparazzi emerged to a paint-smelling kingdom of art. They circled around the roomy facilities together and separately. The most impressing images were the largest ones. The canvas of *The Origin of Life Number One* was filled with female pubic hair, a very concrete or artfully implemented dark-red vulva and a body growing outside the frames along the wall. In the *Origin of Life Number Two* the painting presented an erect penis rising from a dark hairy bush and a male body stretching along the wall. Papparazzi was enchanted by a painting called *The Death* with a crispy white door opening into a pitch-black darkness resembling Kazimir Malevich's iconic *Black Square*. Edna sneaked behind him and whispered:

"Evocative, isn't it?"

"Absolutely! The contrast between life and death has been created splendidly."

"We all leave some sort of mark. The best-case scenario is

leaving it also to future generations. That is – some kind of immortality – what all the living artists are looking for."

Once uttering these wise words, they agreed to make notes of the pictures they favoured. After the evaluation the lovers took a peek out to the deserted street falling abruptly into each other's arms. The passionate kisses were followed by the fiery dance of fingers on those body parts showing on the *Origin of Life Number One* and *Two*. The erotic download erupted. A shadow of camera tube flickered by the window. George Bamby shot photos of the act with steady hand on a continuous pace. A sneak peek at the camera screen brought a wide smile on his face. He left the scene nonchalantly.

After their lovemaking Edna and Papparazzi lay on the floor looking up the ceiling. They saw stars in there.

As Papparazzi was ready to retire for the night at his condo in Pimlico, the phone rang. The caller was Graham Stone.

"Hi! Didn't wake you up, did I?"

"No! But I was just getting ready to…"

"Good! I wasn't sure if I should bring this up with you at this hour. But it felt so important that I decided to pick up the phone nevertheless."

"Okay! What's the deal?"

The chief editor hesitated trying to find the right words.

"Let's put it this way, you have created a quite a stir!"

The photographer was bending upwards with curiosity. Graham went on:

"George Bamby, your local colleague, well known and recognised by you, offered us a package of pictures a couple of hours ago…"

A hundred thousand volts flashed through Papparazzi, slick and slide; his throat was choking and he had trouble breathing.

"What the fuck?"

"The thing is of you having sex on a gallery floor with a mystery lady! Or that is what George wrote in the covering diagram. You have been introduced by your pseudonym."

London Star cut the deal as a protective precaution to their eager beaver, but according to Graham it was clear there would be other medias willing to hit the cash on the table. The subject was too tempting. Having been able to catch his breath, the shooter revealed the true identity of the person he had banged.

"O, it was Edna! You two really hit it off after the Banksy expo?"

"Yes, we did but I could have lived without this episode."

They contemplated the legal side of the pictures.

"You know as well as George Bamby does, with more determination, that the gallery is a public place. Anyone could have passed that window and done the same."

"There is no doubt about it. Of course the situation was very private and intimate. We tried to make sure there was nobody hanging around that window."

"Being a professional, Bamby took his time hiding in the shadows and attacked on cue."

Papparazzi admitted that being the case. He commended Graham on his heads up.

"I might not get any sleep tonight but it was good to hear this now. It gives me time to digest all of this… I won't be caught with my pants down as it would have been the case, having seen those pictures in the morning papers."

"So it was a good thing I phoned you?"

"Of course it was!"

Edna needed to be warned as well immediately. She sounded sleepy when she answered her phone in her one-bedroom flat in

Soho. She got a concise report on having been captured making love and for a moment she seemed to have lost her voice. Papparazzi thought she had fainted in shock.

"Hello? Are you there? Is everything all right?"

"Yes, I am okay. Even though this news blew my mind."

Edna collected herself quickly.

"Listen to me, lover boy! When I started my business, my goal was to become the most adventurous gallerist. Now you have offered me the ultimate escapade! In that spirit I will accredit whatever is coming out with those pictures."

Her wise attitude was the only possible way of seeing things. It had a calming effect on Papparazzi. Maybe he could get some sleep tonight. Edna thought it was essential to let Jo know what had taken place asap.

As a blessed end, they made a decision to keep out of Lesley's Voices of Life expo opening.

"We are stealing too much attention from it at this point, let alone us being present at the opening. The artist and her creations must be in the limelight!"

Papparazzi agreed to his core. As they were saying goodnight Edna cooed on the phone:

"The thing we did on our love-floor still gives me goose bumps."

Hormones were rushing through on the other end of the line as well.

"Well, sleep tight and don't let the bed bugs bite."

The dawn rose upon the world and the first sensational photos were published.

The actual flooding began at the opening of the exhibition. The crowd was so dense that people were unable to fit themselves in. Many of them wanted to see the exact spot in the gallery where Papparazzi and his mystery lady's hot hips had moved in sync. Jo and Lesley did their best evading all the questions. They didn't resent the turnout. They realised that the contemporary art presented in there might not be the main factor explaining the buzz… They kept on being busy in the future as well. The profit in oncoming months was more than Jo and Lesley could have ever even dared to dream of.

Before long the lovemaking pictures were on display everywhere, forcing Papparazzi, Edna, Jo and Lesley to comment on them. The photos with the *Origin of Life Number One* and *Two* showing behind the love scene were the media's favourites. One day the artist sent Papparazzi a text message telling him that she had gotten the best offer ever for them. It was so high that she felt dizzy just hearing it. Although the studio critics' amorous play had upset her at first, she felt now that her dreams were accelerated in a way she couldn't ever have imagined. Owing to an art collector from London, she was able to move to the Caribbean to refine her creativity. After having read her enjoyable news, Papparazzi answered her with gratitude.

The Finn got curious glances from bystanders whenever he was moving in public places. He found it difficult to ignore the gazers and gigglers. Every once in a while he wanted to tell them to get a life. Most of the time he decided not to say anything unless somebody approached him directly. At his home street a casual acquaintance, Wilfred Murphy, tapped his shoulder.

"Hi, Paps! George Bamby pulled the fast one on you, didn't he?"

"Yes, he did, there's no way of denying it. Caught me and my sweetheart with our pants down."

Wilfred couldn't keep a straight face hearing the answer.

"Sorry!"

"No hard feelings. My ex used to call me the master of unintentional humour. Evoking laughter around me doesn't bother me at all."

"You are a celeb now yourself. How does it feel?"

"I'm tasting my own medicine. So far, I have been able to remain behind the camera as a grey eminence. It is not a good thing if my subjects recognise me immediately. It makes my work even harder."

"George was just showing who is the king of the island. He has the attitude of a street urchin."

Papparazzi had heard on the grapevine all kinds of intel about this Hornet of British media. Including his tendency to wipe his backside with the ethical guidelines.

"He has challenged me to some sort of a duel. I have no desire to take this kind of dare."

"That is wise. When are you going to join us in The Gallery Pub? We could have a good chat, and make the world a bit of a better place."

"Let's take a rain check on that. I haven't dared to show my face in that facility since this commotion went off."

"Nobody gives a rat's ass about this kind of trifle!"

"Okay then, maybe I'll pop in sooner than later."

"Well, I look forward to seeing you in there!"

The Gallery had turned out to be Papparazzi's second living room due to its name and close proximity. He had got wasted there. And enjoyed Sunday roasts and other traditional dishes. The decor was of brownish colouring and the furniture was time-marked. The wood panelling, padded chairs and the top shelf filled with books, bottles and other memorabilia created a stagnant atmosphere. The bar was well lit, the mirrors on the back of the bottle shelves gave some added tone to it. The most elegant part of the pub was its gold and black façade. A flower splendour gushed from hanging baskets and boxes on the upper side of the signboard. Papparazzi's most favoured drinking place was in the patio under the sunshade. Once Hubert, the happy-faced bartender, had learned what the Finn's livelihood was, he nicknamed him as Paps. So far, its usage had been limited inside the beer parlour in question. His real name had been pried upon his ID on the bar and on other occasions as well, but it had been too much of a mouthful for anyone to chew on.

That day also came when the messages from the homeland indicated that his gentle moment with Edna, captured by George Bamby, had been published in the media over there. Mandi, Machine, his daughter Julia and Mammarazzi got in touch with him regarding the photos.

The Week magazine sent its representative to sniff the scent of a scandal. Papparazzi had decided to beat around the bush with his answers to the questions sent him by the reporter via email. There was not enough money in the world to get him to enter Jo's Art Gallery for a shooting session. Edna declined as well. She was so up to her throat with the whole shebang that she refused to comment to the reporters, why not comment? Jo and Lesley on the other hand spilled the beans on their behalf. *The Week* got their statements and showed in their two-spread story the photos of Papparazzi bringing his A-game without his camera.

When his ex-wife Raisa caught glimpses of the selected pieces from the story online, she let her sharp tongue waggle in the Nordic outskirts. Some of those chips flew over the land and sea to the screen of Papparazzi's phone.

"Good heavens, you should keep your conjugal visits inside the bedroom instead of doing it in public. You really messed it up this time. Even an uninhibited lady like me was flabbergasted seeing those obscene photos. Get your act together down there!"

STIRRING WILLY-CARD

Papparazzi was enjoying a working lunch with Graham Stone in The Barrowboy & Banker pub. It was located in close proximity of the *London Star* office and was famous for its tasty pies. While forking through one of them, the Chief Editor told him how the rate of paparazzi per capita in London was one of the highest in the whole world.

"The competition is fierce, but on the other hand, there is endless demand for the photos. The more unexpected, intimate and touchy they are, the more sellable they are."

The Finn gave an affirmative nod while sipping his beer. The casually dressed charming gentleman glanced the photographer with twinkling eyes over the table:

"How has your baptism of fire turned out?"

"It's been relatively easy to get into action."

"That's a good start."

Graham understood Papparazzi's ongoing process of building his network of contacts.

"Ultimately we hired you on the basis of your skills. And also, as a foreigner, you have a fresh and exotic point of view of London. To be honest you are everything we bargained for!"

Papparazzi felt good getting positive feedback. Their talk turned to George Bamby, who seemed to have a bone to pick with the newcomer. Papparazzi was delighted with the fact of *London Star*'s rejection to publish the photos taken from the gallery in Marylebone.

"We take firm care of our own. On this occasion it proved costly. We could have made a good profit on them, more times over the purchasing price."

"No doubt about that!"

Media houses in London, including *London Star*, had paid loads of money to Bamby over the years.

"He has never lurked behind the bushes in vain. Every squat has had a price tag attached to it."

"I've heard of him beforehand. At this point he is really putting me in my place."

"I want to make it completely clear to you that we don't expect you to give up on your own ethics. In here you must drive on the left side of the road, but when it comes to your conscience, you can keep yourself on the right track."

"Sounds good. I have no desire to shoot celebs with their children. The only exceptions are the open-minded parents, who have no objection to taking family photos."

"Let's keep it that way."

The Chief Editor had great deal to say about George Bamby's craftiness. On Fistral Beach the Old Timer had lured the owner of the beach bar to give a few wine bottles to the actress Coleen Anderson as a gift. When she walked around holding them in her arms chatting with her friends, a camera equipped with a zoom lens had sung odes in his hiding place. With staggers and weight transfers from one foot to another, it seemed in some of them as if she had been smashed.

"And those drunk pictures were the ones getting published. The stories conveniently enhanced the appearance."

His finest hour came, when the shooter's accomplice had managed to bump into the Prime Minister Stephen Forsythe in a crowd on Parliament Street, making him drop his briefcase and "somehow and out of thin air" there materialised a couple of porn magazines around it. The dark-and-troll-haired Brexit-bigwig had quickly risen to the occasion trying to hide them by packing the goods inside his jacket, but the camera guy on the spot had captured the embarrassing photos of the Prime Minister in a nanosecond."

"The most expensive ones were those photos revealing the naughty content spreading around the briefcase. Were these the most important dossiers the top dog of the nation browsed in the meetings? It caused a sensation, that much I can tell."

Although they knew it was all staged, the joke was hilarious.

"Let's get back to the business," Graham got serious. "In half an hour Kim Harris, one of the journalists in our tabloid, is coming here to interview the equality influencer Lydia Jenner, who wants to share hot news with us."

Once his boss had exited, the scoop shooter ordered more brew. The babble of conversation filled his ears and the smell of the food, his nostrils. The main room was bright, owing to big windows. The bar furniture was traditional and the colour scheme toned down. A padded seat caressed his buttocks. This kind of bush was a good place for a stakeout. His boozing got a new twist, as the young waitress handing the bill cracked a joke:

"Visited any galleries lately?"

Papparazzi snapped back nonchalantly:

"Only my local called The Gallery Pub…"

"I know that beer house! You behaved yourself there, didn't you?"

"Of course I did. Just having a quiet drink, as I'm doing now."

The damsel introducing herself as Gita confessed reading all the Papparazzi-related stories. He revealed his being onto a new story right on the spot as they were speaking. Gita promised to arrange a den for the interview.

"Yes, well, it was good I brought that up."

After the initial formalities, Papparazzi, Kim and Lydia were led up the stairs... to The Gallery! Gita moved the tables at the upper level enabling them to close into their own world. Kim wearing round bluestocking specs set her note-taking stationery and a recorder on the table. Papparazzi took his camera out as well. Their gazes were focused on a brunette female scholar wearing ball-shaped earrings in her ears. She wore no make-up. Her hands fiddled with her handbag as she stated:

"I have been hovering over this for a while now whether I should go public with this obscene postcard I received a couple of weeks ago. Now I have made up my mind to do it."

Lydia dug a card displaying a naked woman parachuting with her bra towards erect penises. On the top of her head was a text: "Cheers to Men!" On the other side of the card was written: "Let's eliminate the pay gaps, focus on what's important!" It was signed by the Brothers of British Airways. The Prime Minister Stephen Forsythe as well as four Union leaders on both sides of employers and employees were members of the brotherhood. The surprising information made Papparazzi and Kim's jaws drop. The shooter knew only the Prime Minister by name but Kim knew all of them well.

"Your Chief Editor asked me to verify the authenticity of these signatures with a handwriting expert. They really are scribbled by this group of gentlemen."

The card turned out to be piping hot stuff on the news front. Releasing it out into the public could have major ramifications.

"Have you any inkling, why they targeted you specifically?" the reporter pried.

"Of course I wondered what their motive was. Do they really at this point – in these blessed times of Me Too – want to remind us that this is ultimately a man's world?"

"We'll see about that! Dirty, suggestive banter is by all means counted as sexual harassment!"

Kim started to kick some serious ass by asking all the possible and impossible questions concerning the postcard. Papparazzi took some random shots waiting for Kim to finish her interview. After that he was able to let out his whole arsenal. The card was photographed accurately from both sides. The texts had to be easily visible to all viewers.

London Star brought up the number one topic to every breakfast table in the UK. The Union leaders were especially reluctant to comment on the case, so the Prime Minister took the post as spokesman of the brothers. The idea of sending the card came to them after a long boozing night in the restaurant of the Strand Palace Hotel. The pen had been pushed into Forsythe's hand and he had been asked to sign a playful card. He had decided to play along, signing the card without looking at what was on the other side. Having done so, he would never have joined in the lively brotherhood. Forsythe apologised for his involvement in the willy-card incident, but refused to resign his post as a Prime Minister due to the scandal. In the oncoming weeks the senders' resignation was in demand on social media and petitions were signed. Forsythe and his accomplices were able to hold on to their seats nonetheless. Although they were keeling for a while. The card invigorated the public speech on equality and women's position in society. Feedback was also sent to the editorial office of *London Star* and the equality influencer. Most condemned the chauvinists in the strongest possible terms, but there were also other points of view as well. "The female in the card is not an object, she is an active selector with plenty of choices."

British Airways made it clear they had no involvement in the brotherhood. The British Parachuters Association shared their warning words. The jumper's equipment was totally inappropriate and unsafe. Since their announcement drew a lot of attention to the association, they couldn't help but advertise their action: "If and when you want to stay clear of the willy-card's naked Barbie, please contact your nearest Jump-club and join the beginners' course!"

HONEY-TRAPPED

Papparazzi had received a hot tip late on Saturday evening. He should saddle up right away, but he wondered whether it was worth the effort. He decided to call Graham Stone although he had serious reservations on timing. Luckily, Graham took it like a professional.

"24/7. That's our trademark, as you very well know."

The tip he'd received concerned a band called The Flashers. They had gone to the Shangri-La Hotel in The Shard building after their latest gig. The members of the band had gotten a sudden idea of posing in their nighties in front of well-known paparazzo. They insisted on getting Papparazzi since his name was on everyone's lips in London. He admitted straight away having no knowledge of the band before this evening. The name rang Graham's bells as they spoke:

"The band in question consists of tuneless groupies, supposedly the new Spice Girls. The foursome tries to mimic the Sex Pistols on the field of the girl pop scene."

"Is it worth my while to shoot them immodestly dressed?"

"That's the point… You never know how immodest their attire actually is!"

"That's why I phoned you. It was uncommonly hard – almost overwhelming – to decide independently whether this will exceed the news threshold."

"It will indeed, so you'll have another nightshift on your hands!"

"24/7. I'm on fire already!"

"You've got the right attitude and sense of action!"

On his way to the skyscraper Papparazzi listened to The Flashers' songs on YouTube. They sounded like muzak in his ears although he wasn't going to reveal the fact on the spot.

Upon arriving he was led to the fiftieth floor by Brigitte, the lead vocalist of The Flashers. All the girls were sexy vortexes with protruding lips and joyful attire. The window wall offered a breath-taking view over the Capital and the surrounding areas. A monumental bed, big enough to fit all four of them to sleep comfortably, was striking. There were bottles of booze and wine standing upright on the tables; shopping bags and purses were scattered on the floor. He almost stepped on a broken sparkling wine glass while browsing the spectacle. The smell of deodorants, perfumes and hair products was stupefying. Probably they had no problems in getting the drugs of their choice either.

They sat on the side of the super-sized bed. Papparazzi confessed, being from the Far-Away-Land of reindeer and elves, he had not enough knowledge of who he was dealing with this time. Therefore, a short introduction took place. The dark-haired and fiery Brigitte was the velvety and also deep throat. The blue-haired Catherine played the guitar and was omnivore when it came to men. The drummer Katy wore her hair in a bun placed on the top of her head, her speciality was cleaning up men's flutes. Mathilde's bass guitar made the listener's bottoms wet and vibrating. Her eyelashes were long and flickered frequently and undeniably sexily. Papparazzi made it clear that he was a professional photographer and the only musical instrument he could play was air guitar. As to the details of his sex life, he was reluctant to reveal more than they had been able to read in the media. The pop artists started giggling after hearing this.

The initial beats of The Flashers were struck, when they had been the fans of the sexiest rock-peacock in England, Sly Turner. They had been at the gigs of the strutting rooster diligently and sieged him at every given chance. And yes: they had had some meth-head sex on several occasions in the back stages, suites, buses and toilets.

"Initially we knew each other just by face but before long we chummed up. We closed our ranks due to Mr Big leaving us high and dry hooking up with his horse-faced Ingrid," Brigitte scolded the rocker.

"She could never give him the ride of his life as we did though!" Katy played along.

The abandoned groupies decided to team up since they had all taken music lessons during their school times.

"One day we will be bigger stars than Sly ever could be. When we are, if he comes to us begging for sex, he'll get no mercy from us! When it comes to him, we are on a love strike!" Mathilde retorted.

"And the pussy boycott sticks!" Catherine assured.

Hitherto they had released one long playing disc called *Gone with The Urges*. The title song was also their biggest hit. At this point they signed up with a flowing-haired and scruffy-bearded manager Jeff Hopkins. The promoter had promised to make The Flashers so rich that they could make enough money to kiss their asses. He launched a brand of scented candles honouring their pussies. The first candle, called This Smells Like Our Vagina, had sold out. The oncoming scent was named This Smells Like Our Orgasm. Their success story was rocketing, but they still had a long way to go on their trip to becoming superstars in the entertainment field. Papparazzi was called in to shoot them on the side of London Bridge in order to smooth their way to the stardom.

The hotties felt like taking off their overclothes and modelling their nighties. They took turns changing in the opulent marble bathroom. Brigitte took the first turn to be caressed by the flashlight flirting in front of the window in her PJs. The most captivating moment came when she bulged her breast out. The sight made Papparazzi glue his sweaty face to the camera. The other girls were dancing, singing and cheering to the wannabe supermodel sucking in sparkling wine and booze like sponges. Next one on the line to exhibit her goodies was Mathilde standing in the bathroom doorway. Her G-strings were so small that they barely covered her private areas. Seductive smile and naughtily bent forefinger highlighted the insinuating erotic download she oozed. Katy wore a see-through nightie wearing only briefs under it. Her perky nipples stuck out. When Catherine emerged from the bathroom, only a towel wrapped around her, everybody blasted with infatuation. She let her nakedness unleash as she capsized on the bed. She announced wearing only Christina Aguilera's floral scent. The shooting wizard hovered around her like a hornet. Suddenly somebody pushed Papa onto the bed. The rest of the princesses of the night plummeted on the bed smothering him under their weight. He submerged under the pillows, duvets and bedspreads. Arms and legs slithered like snakes. The clothes were ripped off. His organic extension, the camera, vanished completely off the map. Whipping movement on the groins, long nails scratching and passionate lips kissing all over...

Profanities flew all over the place around him.

"Undies off!"

"Show us your horn!"

A dark hood in the shape of Katy's tight little bottom

descended on Papparazzi's face. For a second he had forgotten why he was there. Now – in dire straits – he realised how cleverly the girls had honey-trapped him! He started struggling whichever way against his destiny. The maidens fought him with all their might. He got on the winning side only by slumping on the floor in an awkward position. It took almost half an hour for him with his burdens and drags to reach the door and miraculously get out of it wearing only his briefs, lipstick marks on his body. While licking his wounds, curled up at the corridor, a nearby door opened and a sleepy woman's face emerged in the doorway. After hearing what had occurred, she promised to contact the hotel staff. Very soon a gentleman introducing himself as night manager Nicholas Cayne came to his rescue.

"Oh, it's you! Your hormones taking an override again, aren't they?"

The enquirer tried to contain his laughter, while the respondent was holding back his tears:

"Everyone else but me! I've been had big time!"

The manager had difficulties trying to hold a straight face, while listening to Papparazzi's account of the proceedings and helping him to get up from the floor.

"Do you want to stake a claim on the female musicians?"

"I only want my clothes and camera back!"

"That sounds reasonable."

Nicholas knocked on the door without any reaction on the other side. Being so, he opened it with his own key. The room was dark as if the residents were sound asleep. The women couldn't keep silent, they were giggling and buzzing with each other. The night manager turned on the lights and introduced Papparazzi to them:

"This kind of flasher was found in the corridor. Do you know him?"

"Yes, we do. We just had a fivesome with him!"

Papparazzi had difficulties holding it together. He claimed to be the innocent victim in this case – only doing his job. Nicholas was not interested in the incidents in the room as long as nobody blamed anyone for sexual molestation or harassment. No such claim was introduced so he just asked the musicians to return Papparazzi's belongings. His jeans flew on the floor. One at the time other garments emerged too. They had to make a proper search before retrieving the camera. The photographer scrutinised the photos from the screen feeling euphoric, since all the photos were intact.

London Star spread them to the public eye in the morning issues. The photos were praised to be sensual, enticing and bold. Papparazzi had not worked his night shift in vain! After one week the scandal magazine *The Sensation* whacked the readers with a set of more elaborate photos. In those Papparazzi was frolicking naked with the musicians of The Flashers. He had not been aware of the shooting while the game was on. Apparently one of the girls had done so. And now they were cashing in by selling the pictures exclusively to the gossip magazine. At this point, if not before, everyone in Britain and in the whole world had found out what kind of bed-hopper the Finn was. He had given a short briefing of his strangest shooting session ever to Edna beforehand, so the sexy photos blown up on the front pages of *The Sensation* didn't shatter Edna's belief in their relationship to pieces. Pure comedy!

THE NAKED CHEF'S GREAT BALLS OF FIRE

The celebrity chef Ian Betts's French Cuisine restaurant chain had folded. Tens of Ian's French restaurants had been shut down all across the Kingdom. The chain had grown at an exceptional rate over the years. The basic idea was to offer food made with fresh ingredients and passion. Although they had a flying start and cash had poured in, the hard times had been piling up in the passing years. Receiving a phone call in the middle of the night about losing everything, the shocking news made him lose his balance dropping him on his knees.

The famous TV chef gave Papparazzi a beady-eyed glance in Ian's French brasserie in Victoria Street. The furniture of the wide-open space was still intact but the most important factor, i.e. the customers, was scarce.

"Bankruptcy was the worst experience I ever had," he said as he was fiddling with the blue chair's back.

Hearing this was an easy thing to believe. They had arrived at the spot with optimism. The Naked Chef had made Ian a star. Now – down-and-out – he was ready to launch the updated *Naked Chef 2.0*. In the first episode he was going to make a grand entrance – prepare his food having only an apron to cover his nakedness. And wearing sandals honouring the scandal. *London Star* was called in exclusively to follow the shooting of the broadcast taking place in the fall on Channel 69. The only guideline from the Chief Editor was to capture as much of Ian's skin as he could. The photos were to be moved along asap. It was obvious that the next front pages and billboards were marked with Exclusive Stamps.

The ambiance in the kitchen electrified and the smells of food fanned in to noses as Ian begun to hustle at the stove. He had no need to use the flash due to the ambient lighting conditions. The starter was a soup made of stripping tomatoes. They were blanched out of their skin. While Ian was chopping the onions and garlic cloves, Papparazzi got an opening to photograph beside the shooting crew. Ian's back, buttocks, hind legs and calves covered with thick hair ended up in the memory card of his camera. He also got very good pictures from the front as the star collected the groceries. His breast hair was thick as a rug, complimenting nicely his blue and violet patterned apron. With his soup he also conjured some Mozzarella bread. He demonstrated his professionalism well by explaining every step, in layman's terms, spiced with humour, without having to retake almost any of it. He had put an enormous effort into the erotic theme of the opening episode.

After enjoying the appetizer and telling everyone how divine the taste was, he attacked the main course. Papparazzi was not able to capture all of his preparations, but the air was filled with naughty idioms. The broth was seasoned with naked spices, undressed eggs stirred on the pan, nude noodles boiled in the kettle… Papparazzi reached his own climax as well. Even when he was pressing the shutter release, he felt there was something special taking place. In a unique photo, bright light streamed under Ian's buttocks showing the dangling hairy kiwi balls. It was powered up with the chef's glance straight to the Papparazzi's camera over his shoulder. Since then, working proved to be forced. He captured the preparation of the dessert, a fruity and passionate ice-cream cocktail, only a couple of times. When Ian had praised how heavenly everything had been and the TV cameras were shut down, the whole caboodle moved to the parlour to devour the goodies. Strangely enough the crowd gathered in from the front door to have a bite. The service of beverages was kicked off too.

Ian, in his normal attire, shared stories of his past food creations and strolled down memory lane. He had been in the Victoria working his ass off on several occasions and starring the service.

"I've had an unbelievable number of joint pictures taken here! There are so many, I'm in tears just remembering them…"

They were all well aware of the fact that this was the first and the last broadcasting session in this facility. In a couple of days the bailiffs would enter to collect all the personal property. The new entrepreneur would come in trying his luck in there. The *Naked Chef 2.0* would be shot in the studio set from now on.

"Dear friends! This is the last time I'm performing in public wearing only my apron! Next time I'm doing it only in front of my darling Pippa in the privacy of my own home, when having an especially romantic moment."

When Rita Holden, the reporter of *London Star*, took hold of the celebrity chef in order to get a deep interview, Papparazzi exited the restaurant in a full and satisfied state. In a couple of hours there would be a set of photos sent with a click of a button from his Pimlico apartment making eyeballs roll with astonishment globally.

WHEN ALL GOES VERY WRONG

Different versions of *The Play That Goes Wrong* had become very popular in London. Edna capitalized on the same theme, opening a photo exhibition in her two-storey gallery. It displayed photos of Benny Gibson, a trusted shooter of global celebrities. This time the retiring shooter broke the trust – committing a treason. Legions of stars had announced their resentment of the expo and swore they never wanted to be in contact with the American ever again. The bald-headed, bespectacled and moustached geek had travelled around the world shooting the mega concerts of the global stars. He had held expos globally displaying the celebs: sharp, bright and glossy. The gigantic scale and the facial expressions resonated in the pictures beautifully. The visual gunfire hit like the best show.

Everything was the same way even this time but with the crucial difference of something going terribly wrong – really badly. There were forty very carefully selected and signed creations hanging on the walls. Beside every piece of art there was an authentic back stage pass. The opening prices had five digits on them but they anticipated higher offers coming in. Edna took her own commission on the sales, as did Benny. There had not been any sales yet since the expo had been the best-kept-secret of the nation before the opening. The releases and advertising material were to be launched just before the opening. The place buzzed with the invited guests. After the champagne toast and short introductions, the art friends had a chance to freely browse the blunders of the world-famous stars.

Edna had dyed her hair dusky pink. She wore a body-licking marvellous frock with puffed sleeves, smocking contouring her waist and waving skirt. The frock complimented her hair. Papparazzi stood by her side having difficulties keeping his eyes away from the stunner. Edna took lightly Papparazzi's stir-causing sleepover with the babes in thongs at The Shard. It still gnawed on the Finn's peace of mind – especially due to the buzz showing no signs of dying down. As Benny was picking some savoury snacks, he turned to Papparazzi and asked if he wanted to have a closer look at some of the photos on display. The Yankee artist would love to give him some additional knowledge. The offer was too good to be refused. They were already on first-name basis – once they had familiarised each other's careers with scrutiny. Sharing mutual respect went without saying. The blonde's reputation as being a gigolo had stricken him with surprise, albeit he was aware of the true state of affairs. Ergo, Edna and Papparazzi were crazy about each other.

The duo took their time circling the premises until they stopped in front of the picture of the Irish band A4 taken from their World Tour. The foursome was running on the stairs built on the stage straight towards the shooter, when the drummer Adam Hewson fell headfirst trying to stop his fall with his hands. A huge projecting screen on the background reflected the view to the overcrowded audience on the TCF Bank Stadium in Minneapolis. Papparazzi was laughing at him saying: "Of course there is nothing funny in seeing somebody getting hurt but I couldn't help it! Especially, when the other members of the group were scuttling like they were having a poker up their bums.

"The picture was taken at the beginning of their performance. It was supposed to be a dynamic entrance but it was anything but."

During that evening and night, the pain-stricken drummer had hit his barrels so out of rhythm making their gig the shittiest one ever.

The pop icon Nellie Urban was sitting and singing on a giant skull, when one of the supporting wires snapped on a crucial moment sending the red-dressed solo artist flat on her belly down on the stage. In the shot, shocked-faced Nellie reached out to retrieve her fallen mic, the blue background was spotted with light balls. Papparazzi gave his praises to him hitting the jackpot. Lopsided skull was not scary any more. On the contrary, it seemed to be laughing at the incident. The scene was at The O2 Arena in London.

Conor MacPherson, the guitarist of the Australian Low & High Energy, cradled his guitar like it was his baby, while smoke bombs blasted and rockets flared around him. A broken guitar string stuck out between his fingers.

"He continued playing at Western Spring Stadium in Auckland, revealing them playing playback incorruptibly. Conor's reaction was spontaneous – he is squeezing his own little sweetheart after she played a nasty trick on him. He prayed nobody noticed his broken string, even though everyone saw it."

Benny had taken for granted Low & High Energy were always playing live on stage. Later on, the Aussies confessed to using playback occasionally as a backup element.

"Something was broken that December night five years ago…"

"Understood."

The couple stalled in front of a massive portrait near the shop window. The strong-voiced singer Mary Burnett spread her hands frantically on top of a pyramid-shaped ramp construction built on the stage.

"The high heels of her shoes got stuck in the stairs in the middle of the pompous interpretation of the song 'You're the Greatest'. Her intention was to go down with an easy and sexy manner but the Queen of Rock 'n' Roll couldn't move an inch. Her panic escalated making her incapable of singing another note after that."

The picture showed the staff members scurrying with outstretched hands towards her on the stairs on the other side of the construction.

"Once they had managed to help the sexy curlyhead down and she was able to go on with her performance, she never went back on the structure even once during that night."

The episode was played at the SAP Arena in Mannheim.

Miss Wenus used pyrotechnics in her shows. On the popper's Art to The Globe Tour, she performed in the quarter of Bercy in Paris situated in Palais Omnisport. The photo Benny had chosen for the expo was a tight full-length image showing sparkles flying from her boobs and crotch. Beside it was a similar shot after the explosion. Her briskly supported breasts surfaced under her shattered bra and her down-there-hair shone through her holey briefs. None of this was in the original script of the show.

"I bet I'm gonna hear about this revelation for a while! If not the lady herself, her manager or lawyer will be in touch."

"How long did it take you to capture this erotic shot?"

"As usual I can say only fractions of a second. It didn't take long for Miss Wenus to get on top of things. She turned her back on the audience and beelined behind the scenes in order to change into intact clothing."

Edna joined them, stealthily taking Papparazzi's hand. There was no denial it would be polite to let the others hear Benny's tales. In addition, there was about to be a surprise number coming up: the MonaLisa Twins playing Beatles covers acoustically. Later in the evening the sisters would have an electric gig in The Cavern Club. They had been permitted to play the chords right – everything was not supposed to be fumbled up tonight. After hearing 'Here, There and Everywhere', 'Yesterday', 'Till There Was You' and 'If I Fell', Papparazzi was impressed: the skilful, heartfelt playing honoured The Beatles. They were drowned in the twinkle of flashlights. Both Papparazzi and Benny lifted their cameras. Would Mona and Lisa Wagner end up in their future expos? Only time would tell.

Everything has to come to an end, even the opening festivities. The invited audience had clearly enjoyed themselves. After the guests had exited, Edna and Benny were delighted at having at least ten offers on the artworks. Papparazzi believed it was just the beginning. As the American stepped out from the front door to Piccadilly Arcade, the most beautiful English rose pressed herself against the Finn's side.

"Such a wonderful evening!" Papparazzi sighed.

"We still have some sparkly stuff left. Why don't we have one more for the road – maybe even two!"

After sipping them, they left the stage of art and stepped into the middle of the Piccadilly buzz. Chatting joyfully, Papparazzi's arm around Edna's waist, they turned from Piccadilly Circus to Coventry Street. *The Horses of Helios* greeted them radiantly. The music was very loud especially in Leicester Square where they entered in a jiffy. As a matter of fact, the only music playing in both of their ears were 'Till There Was You': "There was love all around, But I never heard it singing, No, I never heard it at all, Till there was you, Till there was you..." The colourful illumination on the plane trees and buildings fulfilled the romantic audio image.

It was only a short walk from the *Agatha Christie Memorial* to Edna's condo in Soho. The close proximity of Rosa's Thai Café at Earlham Street fitted Edna's attire more than fine. Small shops in the basements of the residential buildings were a distinctive feature of her neighbourhood, but everything they saw was a dusty pink colour in their eyes in that magical moment. Edna's one-bedroom flat was tight on space. The bedroom served also as her studio, or rather as a storage room and interim store of the displayed art.

"Some artists' works have practically been forgotten here," she exclaimed taking her dress off.

Papparazzi got undressed as well. The double bed was blushingly narrow and it was not spoiled with too much length, but it fitted them both perfectly. The sundials of the *Seven Dials Monument* hadn't even made a single sound before their hearts pounded in the same pace – vis-à-vis.

A SEXY SPIRAL KICK TO THE FINISH

The English and Italian national teams were going to compete with each other in Brighton. Although it was only an exhibition game before the European Championship Tournament, the mood of a great sport event blew over the whole island. The Three Lions accompanied by their girlfriends and wives had flown in a few days in advance. They were planning on getting some recreation time together. A fenced area had been constructed for them allowing other sun worshipers in. The conditions were strict. Photographers carrying either cameras or smartphones were banned. All the items in question were confiscated before entering the beach and returned on exiting. Papparazzi had learned this the hard way. He was sent to the beach town on the shore by the *London Star* in order to get the most attractive photos of the soccer stars and their partners. The assignment didn't include the game played on the Falmer Stadium. The sports desk would be in charge of the field action.

In the room of the Brightonwave Hotel a thought flashed through. However preposterous the idea seemed it was doable. He wrapped his camera into a plastic bag, placing it in a carrier bag. A foldable shovel was taken from the boot of his car. After that he paced two hundred metres to the beach. The fenced area was deserted allowing him to hide his camera under the seawater-ground stones in the cover of the night. In the end he pulled a beach chair on top of it. It gave him good visibility to the place where the better halves of the players had their water games and bathed in the sun earlier in the day. Having done his deed, he returned to his hotel in order to snore.

At the crack of dawn, Papparazzi strode gallantly inside the gate equipped with his towel and swimming gear. The beach chair had stayed put in the same position where he had set it. The time tick-tocked on sluggishly. The skin scorched, sweat swelled on the surface and water bottle emptied fast. What if the Lionesses never made it there today? The question burned his mind as hot as the blazing sun in the sky. He chose to wait patiently. At midday he was rewarded, when the wags started to pour onto the beach. Also, the goal shark Ernie Tooley's wife Irene was amongst them wearing her thong bikini. She was the number one name making adrenalin cascade in Papparazzi's bloodstream. As Irene and Amy Kelly, the wife of the colossal defender Tony Shilton, started splashing water on each other the photographer pulled up his gear – still covering it with a towel. When Jennifer Gilbert the live-in girlfriend of the winger Ashley Gane joined in the splashers, Papparazzi rushed up with his camera tube uncovered and started shooting on speed fire. The closest sun bathers were startled and let out sounds of wonderment. One pitch-voiced Kiri Te Kanawa was amongst them. The security guards from the gate rushed towards Papparazzi. He also got busy. He couldn't be bothered with towels, flip-flops and other paraphernalia. The camera was the most important load he was carrying. He leapt like a tiger over the fence contraption and cannonballed along the beach breathing heavily. He kept up the same pace until he reached the hotel. Before that he had double checked nobody was after him. He had a strong feeling of being able to shake his pursuers. An ice-cold shower helped to set his heart-rate back to normal. A fast-track processing to the photos, cover letters attached and then the shots were sent to the right email address in London. In half an hour Graham phoned him back stoked.

"The sexiest bikini team I've ever seen! Your reward will be fit for a king! The whole kingdom will crap themselves at seeing these shots!"

And it's also the case in here. The next day the wags asked Papparazzi to shoot them on their shopping trip to the Brighton shops. He made a small fortune out of those photos as well. *London Star* was singing praises in their feedback. The most heart-warming WhatsApp message came from Edna: "My darling chunk of gold! You have gained sovereignty of Brighton!"

On the night before the oncoming match event, Papparazzi celebrated his accomplishments in Maggie Mae's bar with Rob. Being a soccer fan to the core, not only the Three Lions but also Fulham FC, although at this point he resided further east, in Shadwell.

"My pad is so tight that I have to sleep standing like a horse."

Rob had dyed his hair salt and pepper colour. The opaque highlight made him look younger.

"I went to a rejuvenating surgery due to my break-up with my girlfriend. We were together for six months, but the love chemist had left out some essential ingredient of our relationship."

"You'll find the right one eventually."

"Perhaps, perhaps not."

Rob was wearing the England national team jersey and shorts – not in any way the only ghost-pale attendant in the hot spot where music got louder and the atmosphere intensified by the minute. The crowd was getting electric shocks, or that's what it seemed, when Mrs Tooley breezed in with her canvas sail taut and incredible bootie. Rob kicked gently at Papparazzi's ankle under the table.

"Do you think we'll see some shiptease tonight?"

The rascals burst out with laughter and toasted again. A couple of wags joined Irene at the bar, when she was making an order: Terry, the wife of goalkeeper Elliot Beck, and Harriet, the wife of captain Justin Gish. They radiated beauty and self-confidence around the bar. As if angels had descended in the middle of the pub crowd. Gazes pierced through them, autographs were asked and given. Papparazzi's lamp was turned on. A semi-smile on his lips, he whispered to Rob's ear something cagey. Rob's facial expression went sugary. The pale ghost stood up and headed his way towards to the all pressed and powered lady-trio. Once he was passing them, he lowered his shorts to the half-mast, the tabloid shooter snatched his camera up and did his magic with it. Irene, Terry and Harriet did see the bare butt whizzing beside them and the flashlight gleaming behind the window table, but their only reaction was a giggle – they showed no sign of shock or nervousness whatsoever. The shooting session was over within seconds – most of the barflies had not noticed anything out of ordinary taking place. Papparazzi emptied his glass and was making his departure with the camera hanging around his neck.

"Papparazzi! What's the rush? Don't you want to have a closer look at what we purchased yesterday?" Irene fluted.

Papparazzi mumbled vaguely something in response and excused himself before the sweeties could blink their eyes. Rob used the facilities making his escape unnoticed as well. The duo met at the Brightonwave Hotel and chose together the sensational pictures to be sent to the paper. They aroused well-earned praises having enough time to make their way in to the gameday's printed issue! The Tooley Mooney startled the whole Kingdom from monarchs to beggars. The culprit mooning to wags was searched high and low, a hefty reward following the finder. Rob signed it off with interest revealing himself in a living interview featuring all available representatives of the media. In his opening speech he apologised for having stolen the media attention from England's home victory of 2–1.

"This time me and the wags took the limelight from the players!"

Why on earth Rob had pulled his stunt?

"It was just a drunken whim… Papparazzi, the devil in a human form, managed to be on the right spot on the right time – and the rest is history!"

After returning home, the Finn received an uplifting text: "Hi! Well done, buddy! I would have done the same, having been in Brighton myself! Yours, George Bamby."

What was all that about?

MARCHING ON TO MADAME TUSSAUDS!

Papparazzi was sleeping like a baby, when Graham's phone call woke him up at the crack of dawn. The chief apologised for his early call before going into the business.

"There is a major event taking place at Madame Tussauds. Could you make it there by seven?"

Curly took a sneak peek at his watch, it was quarter to six.

"No problem getting there, but the wax cabinet isn't even open yet, is it?"

"*London Star* is entrusted with an exclusive story gig. Our reporter James Webster living in Bloomsbury has promised to join in with you. His pen is fast and fluid."

Papparazzi wondered once again what was the emergency needing a tabloid's attendance.

"The most modest request has arrived from the eminent level," the chief editor begun with his enigmatic voice continuing in a more decisive tone: "Or in better words, we got our marching orders."

And that was the end of the matter.

An interesting sight was in front of him on the Marylebone Road: Madame Tussauds without queues. In front of the main entrance there was an impeccably dressed reporter waiting. James was astonished at the early morning assignment too.

"The press infos are usually held during office hours." James sighed.

"We are on the verge of excitement!" Papparazzi gloated.

The Managing Director David Buckheimer galloped to them. Once they had shaken hands, he gestured them in. They arrived at the royal family in a jiffy. The sight made the guests' jaws drop. The wax figures of Prince Richard and Duchess Betty were moved away from the side of the Queen, the Duke of Edinburgh, the Duke and Duchess of Cambridge. The figures of Richie and Betty were standing in the forefront, the others stood in their usual places behind them. Betty wore a stylish green dress and Richie had a blue suit on. He held his right hand inside his jacket in a Napoleonic style.

"I understand your astonishment, dear sirs! In an hour we are going to announce an official bulletin. As of today, Richard and Betty are not part of the royal family collection!"

This was how Madame Tussauds reacted to the couple's announcement of opting out of the British Court. The situation was so exceptional that it made Papparazzi's feet itch for action. The shots were flooding in. Hold on! Did Betty's eyelid stir a bit? That wasn't possible! The morning fatigue must have been playing tricks on him. Until the same figure obviously changed her weight from one foot to another and the one beside her began moving as well. Richie and Betty took turns in commenting:

"We do not want to leave! Could some kind person come to our aid?"

Both James's and Papparazzi's jaws dropped. What the heck! The plot was revealed once the couple lost their cool. David joined their joy too.

"Gentlemen! In the flesh today – Prince Richard and Duchess Betty!"

The named rushed to greet the newspapermen.

"Since we happened to be in London and heard of the plans Madame Tussauds had, we decided to come to the scene to share our feelings," Betty said. Richard nodded his head beside her.

James sharpened his pen and set his recorder rolling.

"So, how do you really feel?"

"We were just kidding when we claimed resenting the removal of our figures. We totally comprehend why the wax museum had no other choice in these circumstances," Richard replied.

David cut into the conversation by announcing that they had removed the figures from the collection the evening before.

Papparazzi was only half listening to Richard and Betty's comments since he was totally focused on photographing the star couple. These opportunities were rare and far apart, when one was able to get this close to aim for them. The couple was visibly in a very good mood, the smiles were almost tattooed on their faces. After finishing his part of the gig, he began browsing the wax figures of the royals. Although Margaret Thatcher had been called the Iron Lady, the most Ironed English Lady in his mind was the Queen, wearing her regal garment, her bright eyes staring straight at him. The crowned head seemed to came to life as also the hand of the Duke of Cambridge moved a bit. Papparazzi was so startled that he crapped his pants. Were there more royals present in the wax museum? David's hand landed softly on the shooter's shoulder. The boss roared with laughter together with Richard, Betty and James.

"Our staff couldn't help pulling your leg a bit. Step forward behind the figures, Kiera and Wilfrid!"

They did as they were instructed. David complimented his multi-talented staff's ability to manage a magic trick. Wilfrid was a tall and gaunt youngster and Kiera was not spoiled in size, which explained how their trick-playing had been a complete success.

David thanked the representatives of *London Star* for their visit as he was shooing them off. He still had some heart-to-heart discussion to conduct with the couple. James had one more question he wanted to ask as a blessed end.

"You have shared on social media your need of less media attention and more privacy than it is possible to get in your current position. How come you two are moving to Hollywood where there are – if possible – more paparazzi per capita than in London?"

Richie let the facts to speak for themselves.

"But there are no Papparazzis as far as we know – not yet anyhow!"

They all burst out in laughter. Papparazzi took the remark as a major tribute to his achievements. Whether he had passed the noticing threshold of the couple on his photographic merits or with other means had no bearing in it. At the moment of goodbyes, the boss of the place made his last revelation.

"Since Betty and Richard are one of the most beloved couples here, they will still have a role in our museum collection, when we have a better overview of what lies in the future."

"We'll be back!" the couple swore.

When James and Papparazzi entered the front entrance of the building, they saw people queuing having drinks from their water bottles.

"The heat is on!" the wordsmith blurted.

Papparazzi was just saying something appropriate, when he solidified into a totem pole. On the side of the nearest tourist bus waved… Richie and Betty! This was more than he had bargained for! The working couple got simultaneous text messages with the same content: "It's David again! The ones waving at you are professional actors who pulled on the masks of Duchess Betty and Duke Richard in order to mess with you. Thank you for visiting us and welcome back to Madame Tussauds!"

The scarf guy took some pictures of the tricksters as well. They could be of use at some point. He offered James a ride to the office. The whacking pictures and soul-stirring story would soon see daylight.

ABSTINENCE IS THE GREATEST PLEASURE

In the TV show *Temptation Island* couples test, on a paradise island, whether their intimate partnership can survive the sweeter taste of forbidden fruit. The famous Morning TV host Lewis Greenway wanted to show, in the spirit of the series, how solid his own marital status was. His spouse Shannon encouraged him to embrace the challenge. When Lewis was making a documentary on the filthy rich Brits living in Marbella, he was given a great opportunity to take it on. Lewis had asked Papparazzi to join him as his private photographer on the site – the whole world and his wife had to be able to see, how he persevered in front of the temptations. The tabloid photographer was accommodated at the Benabola Hotel in Puerto Banus. He was there at his own risk. He would sell the photo collection to the highest bidder. According to their plan during the days, Lewis was stuck to his doc visiting the opulent houses and the business premises of the wealthy Brits. The twosome would be active in the evenings and nights even when needed. When and if Lewis scored, i.e. he did find a female companion, he would keep Papparazzi posted by sending him text messages of his amorous activities. They had chosen three places to visit where a man with Lewis's celebrity status would find himself hot companions. The places were the Ocean Club, Linekers Bar and Club Olivia Valere. The latter two were also mentioned in the documentary.

    When the duo arrived at the Ocean Club after dark, it was filled with wealthy partygoers and achievers willing to celebrate.

The view from the saltwater pool opened up to the Mediterranean. Champagne was sprayed around in the formula-one-race-winner style. Designer brand purses and diamond jewellery flashed and the coiffures touched perfection. Lewis and Papparazzi got the royal treatment, since all the PR people were welcomed, but having someone with Lewis's global status in the premises was priceless. The best ad ever! They were welcomed with frosty cocktail glasses and bottles of Cristal champagne. Papparazzi gave his bottle to Lewis with honours. Obviously, Lewis needed it more than he, since the TV face was the one trying to lure the most flamboyant moth of the pool area in his net. The knight of the night had a well-groomed outfit on too. The most eye-catching feature of him was his white shirt with the unbuttoned collar. He also wore stylish swimming trunks under his linen trousers. This was something Lewis had revealed as they walked together to the coastal bar. The camera guy stood willingly in the background at this point. Lewis vanished with his liquidated load into the vortices of the partygoers, sun-loungers and beds.

During the passing hours Papparazzi caught only few glimpses of Lewis. It was obvious he had a lot of buzzers and autograph seekers gathering around him. The TV star had also caught his fair share of champagne drizzles on him. One of the lassies was licking it off from his bare-stripped chest passionately. The partygoers emptied the bottles super-fast. A cracking sum of money was going down the drain in the eyes of Papparazzi's mind. Nobody else gave a rat's ass of thinking it – the action was so light-hearted and randy. By the shadow of the palm tree an evergreen of the Finnish band SIG rose as his earworm: "Sex, sex, the epidemic of this century. It's making us all crazy!" How well the song fitted in the ambiance of the Ocean

Club! Techno music was banging hard at this point. All sorts of entertainers gave amusement during his long hours of waiting. The break dancers were a joyous sight, flexible like willow branches in the wind. He ordered a few shots making sure he was in working order at all times. This gig was like any other one, it wouldn't be spoiled by excessive boozing.

His phone vibrated as a sign of an arriving message. Lewis asked Papparazzi to join him in a jiffy, a situation was on at the one of the sun beds. The shooter got good coordinates. Lewis was lying down embracing a champagne-blond-dyed bombshell fitting the bill, introducing herself as Mizzy.

"We have really hit it off with Mizzy here!"

The kitten purred beside him with content, having nothing against taking her picture with Lewis. Papparazzi got into action with his gear. In a couple of minutes he was ready to leave the couple sucking on their drinks and each other. It was no wonder he was struck with a sudden exhaustion, since the night had stretched itself into the wee hours of the night. Papa Lewis on the other hand had the endurance of a young stallion. The gifts of happiness don't come equally.

In the morning, Papparazzi got a full account on the happenings of the night. "After you left, we dug ourselves under the pillows making sure nobody could see us, having a foreplay for about half an hour. Once she had taken off her bathing suit and I was getting in doggie style, I started to have second thoughts beginning to almost wail, how I was not going to play such a low trick on my beloved wifey-pooh, so I pulled my doodle out of the danger zone. It was right in the lips i.e. it was a close call... Mizzy really tanned my ass. She called me cuckold and other names. End of story!"

Papparazzi acknowledged the message stating that he had

passed his first temptation with flying colours. There would be more ordeals up and coming so it was not the time to air out his accomplishment on the previous night. Lewis agreed. "Now I have to get rid of my hangover with a shower and breakfast, so I must bid farewell!"

At midday Papparazzi drove in his rental car to lunch on the Polo House at the Golden Mile. The restaurant owner James Hewitt, Princess Diana's former riding teacher and lover, was in the habit of socializing with his customers. The Brit himself wanted to be mostly commemorated as being an entrepreneur trying to make a fresh start instead of his past with Diana. The photographer ordered salad and white wine recommended by the waiter to go with it. While Papparazzi was waiting for his lunch, he reminisced over Diana's short but very colourful life. Although the star of the Princess shone also in Finland, only coming to England had given him the final insight into what an impact the beauty had truly made to her fellow islanders. None of the words were enough to describe it, but the sea of flowers in front of the Kensington Palace after Diana's demise shouted loud her relevance to the Brits. The English Rose had never withered; it still bloomed inside people's hearts. Mr Hewitt appeared on the scene along with his lunch. This time Papparazzi was not the first in line to take out his camera. Women were especially keen to have their picture taken together with James. Papparazzi shot some pictures himself with his mobile phone as the ladies' man approached his table. Papparazzi showed his true colours and asked him straightforward what was going on with his love life. This wasn't the right time to beat around the bushes, so he had to get straight to the hottest question.

"I haven't got a lady-friend at this point. Which magazine is this going to?"

"In some tabloids... only. With a small print..."

"Yeah right!"

That was all they had to say to each other. Papparazzi was adamant James didn't believe anything he was saying, which suited him perfectly. The food was good too. The environment was intimate and ambient. One could have taken a table on the outside under the sunshade as well. Most of the clientele was female. How many of them had dreamed in their subconscious mind of James giving them the eye? The place was oozing that kind of romance. The conclusion was clear: the odds were on James's side, when having no steady female companion at his side. There was no shortage of abundance for having a fling.

By nightfall Papparazzi was loitering in the bar of an Italian restaurant La Pappardelle located along the main shopping street. A few shots later he got a little chattier with the bartender Lorenzo. The Italian had an excitingly high-pitched voice.

"There are a lot of available women around here. A male paradise!"

"I have noticed this myself as well. You can see a lot of celebs here too."

"Yes, they are piling up here!"

Right after, the server named the celebrities he had bumped into over the years: actors Meryl Streep and Pierce Brosnan, director Spike Lee, boxer Mike Tyson, artists Ed Sheeran and Ariana Grande, Spice Girls in different times and contexts... The list was long enough to make Paps give his email address to Lorenzo in order to have him put the names in writing and deliver them to him. He vouched to send them to him at some point, maybe the day after tomorrow or the following week.

"Paparazzos have no need ever to leave this place empty-handed!"

"Hardly me either since I'm known as the one and only Papparazzi," he introduced himself.

"By the way, the introduction of your trade was made in my home country Italy. Everything got started in Federico Fellini's film *La Dolce Vita*."

"I know the film well. It has dwelled in the back of my mind all these years. It might be the reason for my choice of profession."

"Well, are we going to see you shooting here again some time?"

"Who can tell. Maybe I will."

The next shot was on the house. And the next one. The alcohol hummed inside his head. At that point he remembered agreeing with Lewis not to hang around the party hole tonight, the TV guy had promised to text him when the momentum was on. This way Papparazzi could be the most efficient. He had to get to the hotel asap and be prepared for the action, no time for boozing any more. Fortunately, Linekers was only a short walk away. In the darkness of the night Lewis was waiting for him cuddled up with a milk coffee coloured sex bomb named Brown Sugar. Her clothes were licking her like syrup on top of brown sugar. Lewis was also well presented in his Hawaiian shirt and loose pants. They were kissing passionately. Brown Sugar asked the DJ to play The Rolling Stones' hit 'I Can't Get No Satisfaction'. The choice was excellent – they would never get the sexual gratification… Which was something the beauty was totally unaware of at this point. They danced on the floor as wildly as did everyone else. Papparazzi captured the fierce vortices of the lovebirds in fifteen minutes.

Papparazzi received a very interesting reference from the celeb in the middle of his beauty sleep. Lewis had escorted his maiden fly to his residence in Hotel Park Place. "Our romping in the bed in my suite climaxed, when Brown Sugar was slowly and surely mooning her exuberant butt on the top of my face. At that point I was able to cough out my pivotal no. She froze on the spot wanting to make sure if she had heard me correctly – that I wasn't willing to keep up our encounter. I nodded my head like a bubblehead. I have never seen anyone vanish into the thin air so fast."

What an *Arabian Nights* story all over again! He was making stronger and stronger appearances in having to make it with flying colours however seductive the temptresses were coming his way. After having acknowledged the message, he decided to tackle his hangover by taking a stroll in the main shopping street admiring the yachts. The golden rule of the luxury marina seemed to be that the bigger and the most magnificent yachts were berthed to the nearest spot for easy access to close-by services. On the subject of cars, their brands were able to dazzle the eyes: Ferrari here, Lamborghini there, Bentley everywhere... He also slipped inside the luxury stores. Maybe he could find something unforgettable for Edna. In the Gucci shop he found the former boss of English Championship team Birmingham City, Karren Brady, who after following Papparazzi's browsing commented: "Listen! When and if you have to ask the price, there is no way you can afford it!"

A big burden fell from his shoulders. He was certainly not in the right place at the right time.

"I think I'll buy something nice for my sweetheart from the Malaga Airport, since I'll be returning to the foggy island tomorrow."

"You do that! Get some bling-bling to show off and something sweet for her mouth," Karren tipped.

Although she had his hands full of shopping bags from other stores, it didn't stop her from purchasing more. A wealthy lady like her could never have too many handbags in her closet. She used the scarf guy as her Sherpa coming out from the store without hesitation. A late lunch and an afternoon nap were more than welcoming after such a demanding task. The waiting game was on: what would his last night in Marbella bring along?

In Olivia Valere there was an awesome groove going on. Lewis was paying amorous attention to the Queen of Marbella, while she was dancing among the crowd and sometimes even on the tables. A passionate and fiery flamenco show worked splendidly as one number of the eventful night. At the end of the performance the famous guy got familiar with the lady by offering her a drink. The party queen was an eye magnet in her ruffle dress, her hair hanging loose. The man of the world had dressed for the part too.

"You ooze sex and danger the way Carmen does in the opera," Lewis began his easy-going small talk.

"The word of caution is in order, my dear senor! Many men have burnt their fingers falling in love with me…"

Now it was the other party's attitude in place! Persuading an elusive lady to his side and his bed was a pleasurable challenge the playboy grabbed greedily. More drinks, something stiff for both of them! Once they had boozed enough to make their heads spin, Lewis summoned Papparazzi to join in. Before long they were in a position to be posing intimately with his newest conquest in front of the photographer. The Finn had arrived on the spot in good time in order to snoop around the night club and its surroundings. He finished his job while the subjects were sharing hugs and hot, moist kisses. Thank you and bow!

The early message from Lewis had become the highlight of Papparazzi's day. "We went to the condo of the Spanish Senorita to play some bonding games. It was perfectly equipped for the task. I was so drunk I totally forgot the safe-word we had agreed beforehand. Once I was in such a quagmire unable to move myself and losing the hope of avoiding an intercourse, I retrieved my memory to the keyword – Äteritsiputeritsipuolilautatsijänkä – and burst it out of my mouth. You told me about the swamp having that name in Lapland. Carmen's disappointment was tangible. Especially when I sighed my remark of abstinence being my greatest pleasure, I had to make a fast getaway! Handcuffs, whips and other paraphernalia flying behind me…"

Lewis's adventures as a womanizer aroused interest in the tabloids. The pictures sent to the winners of the bidding contest were attached with provoking texts. This was something the island nation had not seen in ages – at least not since the *News of The World* had ceased to exist. Lewis trusted totally the professionalism of the whole process wanting not to interfere in the visual material as well as leaving the texts without proof reading. After they had been burst in the covers and headlines, Papparazzi received the tragic news on his mobile phone: "Hi, its Lewis here! Or should I speak of myself as a reborn contemporary Casanova? I'm listening to Chopin's funeral music at my home, scattering ashes on top of me and screwing a wine bottle open. Shannon lashed out at me after seeing those sensational pictures in the papers. I had gone too far with them. By no means, had she encouraged me to test the limits of our relationship that way, but rather more delicately with things like flirtation and naughty words at the most to the frumps. Shannon is so devastated that she is now filing for a divorce!"

The drunkard sent several messages with the same contents to the camera guy. The final one spoke in a loud voice: "I just should have pushed it on in Marbella!"

NAUGHTY LITTLE OPEN HOUSE IN ILFORD

A renowned TV realtor Rita Thompson opened the door of an apartment to Papparazzi in Ilford. They shook hands and hugged. The fifth-floor unique apartment in Axon Place was about to be listed and Rita wanted to give *London Star* the first preview. Media exposure could help make the sale. The artist Fanny Willis had left her mark in the one-bedroom condo.

"In this case it's like selling a piece of art rather than a flat," Rita emphasized.

The telephone interview with the reporter had already taken place, therefore Papparazzi's main task was to take the pictures making the place look as sexy as possible. Rita, a dark-haired and voluptuous woman, would have fulfilled all the conditions herself, even if the flat had been painted white all over. Papparazzi had first seen her popping into fame at early age with her TV show *Fixing and Selling with Rita*. In that one Rita helped the homeowners, who were jammed trying to sell their shoddy houses. Two grand, a paint brush and a hammer to the owners, the junk in the recycling or to the junk yard was her prescription in all its brevity to make a quick sale. Her forte was her quick wits, good sense of humour and determination. She was able to make even the laziest of owners work their butts off during the seven-day-period.

Without further ado the amazon and the camera warrior proceeded into the bedroom, the erotic colouring of which made Papparazzi's jaw drop. Rita just couldn't help but laugh seeing his stupor. The headboard of a king-size bed was decorated with a winged heart, on the ceiling was another stylised one illuminated with spotlights. On the right-side wall of the bed there was an immodestly dressed woman holding a smoking gun, a bullet was in the air further up. The lady had a dramatic expression on her face, clips on her nipples and the flames under her waist. The sinful red drapes and the ebony blinds brought their own tone in the sight. The window bench was wide enough for lovemaking. The Finn was so flabbergasted that Rita had to kick his ass into gear. Soon the camera shutter clicked at the same pace with Rita's eyelashes. The low-cut neckline of her multi-coloured dress was more than appropriate in the ambiance of the room. She came to life in front of the camera anyway.

The kitchen had been transformed in the hands of the artist into an erotic minibar. On the wall the duo was greeted by a 1950s bare-breasted pin-up girl holding her forefinger up. The message was immediately clear to the connoisseur Papparazzi: "Come here, bad boy!" There were embossed fruits, a popcorn machine and a kettle laid on the red-hot countertop. A phallus shaped tap was erected on the top of the sink. In the open plan space was also the living room with a radiating coffee bean painted on the floor aka a Finnish church boat. In a visible position there was also a folding screen made of glass showing a bombshell in a maid's dress hugging a feather duster. Papparazzi asked Rita to pose beside the figure. The arrangement worked like a charm.

In the bathroom there was a churning and glittering fountain-shaped installation on the top wall of the in-built sink and bathtub. The rest of the walls were covered with a flaming yellow-red mosaic tiling. Papparazzi's favourite photo was the one where Rita caressed the silk ribboned roses and skulls framing of the mirror.

Once the round was finished, they sat at the bar counter to have instant coffee. The boldness was seen in the stools as well: their butts sank easily between meaty sugar lips.

"What does your gut instinct say about this flat's sellability, when the audience gets to marvel at the story with the luscious pictures?"

"It is hard to say. At least it is noticeable!"

Rita winked and said:

"Aren't you renting yourself at the moment? Now you have an opportunity of the lifetime to make a deal and live as the playboy you are claimed to be! Let's get the paperwork going and you can sign them right here and now. I have a mandate to make the deal, if the buyer is ready to pay the listing price."

The request swept over Papparazzi making him spill his coffee mug on the quartz countertop.

"It's a toughie… What is the artist asking?"

"376,500 pounds. If you compare it with the most expensive artworks, it's a bargain!"

Now the coffee was flowing down his hairy legs, since Papparazzi was wearing shorts and T-shirt due to the hot summer day.

"Damn! I'm just like Elizabeth in *Keeping Up Appearances*! I'm getting all nerves being around you!"

Rita passed a wipe to the nervy man in order to wipe off the spillage. She was having giggling convulsions. While Papparazzi was cleaning the mess up, he spoke out his hesitant reaction to the suggestion.

"Although I am a patron of the arts and not in anyways a prune, this is too much for me. Besides I do enjoy living in Pimlico, the situation works perfectly for me. Ilford is too far out from downtown."

"I must admit the proposal was not a serious one…"
"But you would sell it in a jiffy, if I took the bait."
"No doubt about it!"

After the flat was listed, Papparazzi got a postcard from Rita with a glowing coffee bean on the front, on the back was a feminine scribbling; a joyful message: "Hello, camera hog! A sunny message from Ilford. The erotic condo in Axon Place is sold! The buyer made an offer Fanny couldn't refuse. The investor living inside you is crying over the possible rise on the value you have lost. Let's keep on rowing! Yours, Rita T."

UNDER THE SPELL OF SIREN

The dark and spicy singer Sointu Virta was looking for a new rhythm to her career. She and her spouse/manager Aava had flown to the island of Lesbos for six months. The breakaway was also an adventurous second honeymoon to them. In Lesbos love between women was a natural thing. Thanks were due to the poetess Sappho who lived in 600 BC. Many of her erotically tuned verses were written to women. Only one of her poems – Hymn to Aphrodite – survived to posterity after the later day moralists systemically destroyed her production. As Sointu and Aava's excursion to the Greek Island was coming to an end, they had a lot of tales they wanted to share with the media. The interviews were made online but *London Star* wanted Papparazzi to fly over. The photographer had a dinner date with the couple in a Mytilene restaurant To Kastro. On the recommendation of Aava and Sointu the curly chose swordfish as his main course. The lovebirds also preferred the seafood. They ordered bottles of red and white house wine to wash the food down. They all agreed to love Greece with all their hearts. The pleasure of speaking Finnish after a long time gave them more joy. In between the meal, the couple went over their experiences in Lesbos. The first couple of months had gone like time had wings although they didn't have very much to show off on the front of creativity. Things had taken a new turn once an Athenian songwriter Grigor Panzanikis had made a sudden appearance in their lives. The encounter bore the resemblance of singer Arja Saijonmaa's and composer Mikis Theodorakis's fatal meeting decades ago. Grigor had arrived on the island wanting to have some time to clear his head after a long tour. They met for the first time at a beach restaurant in Petra. Even though he had taken a vow not to get mixed into the music-making, Sointu and Aava had got him thinking differently. On that very night in the pitch-black night under the full moon and stars they had looked for a common tune in the beach. Grigori's hands played the guitar like an angel.

"It's a pity we didn't write anything down at that point. The music he played was so wonderful and unique," Sointu fretted.

"When Grigor heard Sointu's singing for the first time, he blurted out immediately the magic word: Siren! That became the keyword to our cooperation. Grigor composed and wrote lyrics to Sointu for the rest of his vacation," her blond spouse rejoiced.

At this point they had five or six songs waiting for the last touch before releasing them on her new album *The Siren*. They still needed the same amount in order to finish the album. The new one would be published under her own label No Harm Done.

"The title track caresses the ears. Every time I sing it my heart-rate goes up. Although the sirens have a dangerous reputation in the Greek mythology, I'm representing their beautiful and enlightened features."

After the meal, Papparazzi took pictures of Sointu and Aava in the restaurant and the streets nearby. He didn't want to clear the desk since the International Women's Festival was about to culminate the next night to the concert Sointu was giving in the fishing village Skala Eros. That was Papparazzi's main photo gig in Lesbos. After taking their time wandering around the town, they spotted the Motel Boutique Club where they had their last drinks for the night. The chatting went on more smoothly. Aava and Sointu had lived on multiple parts of the island. They were especially familiar with Mytilene and Petra in the first months of their residence there, until they had found Skala Eressos, the birthplace of Sappho. The Sappho Hotel had become their favourite although they had also used some other facilities there.

"You can be honest and free as being who you are. In there you can party, do yoga, surf, walk hand in hand on the beach, see movies and fashion shows, lunch and dine in tavernas and so forth. It is a paradise on earth for us. The International Women's Festival is the tastiest cherry on the cake," Aava reported.

"The event has regular visitors. The friendship and love is rippling in the air," Sointu described.

They got Papparazzi's full attention. There was no doubt that their trip had fit the bill and even exceeded it. A good break from the everyday routines would do a world of good to all of us... to him and Edna perhaps? Why not? On further reflection it was hardly a possibility – they both were wrapped up in their work. His thoughts were cut off by a giant yawn. He had no choice but to turn in to bed as he was too slumberous to do anything else. They all spent the night in the capital of the island, Sointu and Aava at their friend's condo and the camera guy in the Blue Sea Hotel. The lovebirds would rush to Skala Eressos at the crack of dawn. The preparation for the evening show was Sointu's priority. She wanted her performance to be as energetic and spectacular as it ever could be. In addition, they were supposed to pick Grigori, the minstrel of the concert, up from the airport at midday. The shooter would make his own way to the location. He was well aware that the timing of the journey was of the essence, since the fishing village was on the other side of the island.

Papparazzi arrived to the festival grounds in the nick of time, as the show was about be starting on the stage built in connection to the Parasol Beach Bar. Sointu in her long fluffy short-sleeved dress grabbed the mike and started singing. The guitarist caught fire when 'No Harm' echoed in the air. The spotlights followed them and the coloured lights throbbed in the rhythm of the music. The biggest fans were packed in front of the construction. Everybody else was rolling as well. At first the shooter stood back in order to get his job done. Once the set had proceeded into 'Paparazzi' by Lady Gaga and the song most remembered from the film *A Star Is Born* called 'Evergreen', he advanced nearer to the stage. Sointu took off some of her clothing in the heat: under her disposable skirt was a mini-length wrap dress that was soon thrown on the stage. She continued her performance wearing a tube dress with newspaper print on it. Pappy was checking his accomplishments in the middle of the crowd. The broad black eyeliner, long eyelashes and her crimson lips were clearly visible in the close shots. Her curls were drawn on the other side of her head in Greek style crowned with a band. Large earrings glittered in the lights. Not bad!

Eventually the new songs took their turn in the performance. 'The Eternal Fire', 'Island of Love', 'The Hot Sands of Arcadia' and 'The Golden Lyre' made the listeners go wild. During them Aava, dressed as a siren, tiptoed in between Grigori and Sointu. The classic Greek style dress had a golden belt and a golden buckle on her shoulder. Her sandals were laced up to her knees. Her hair had been curled into the same fashion as her spouse, the band on her forehead was spot on. Bright eyes with their dark brown shadowing on the corner bones and rose-coloured lipstick complimented the fabulous style. Aava and Sointu slapped each other's bums enthusiastically between the songs. The grand finale was getting on. Aava murmured to the mic: "The Siren!"

Once the playing started, Aava turned on her heels and retreated with an erotic swing on the rear left in the dark shadows.

The crowd was so loud that Papparazzi could hear just one word here and there, and the chorus: "Siren, a voice on the sea, enchants you. Bring yourself closer, to the passionate vortexes, my darling…" The song had hit material judging by the people singing the chorus with passion. Suddenly the music hit a dead end leaving Sointu to stand in the limelight all alone. She tore her dress away revealing her astonishing naked body to all people. She straddled behind the mike stand with her gaze pointed into the sky and hands spread at her sides. The camera made love with the sight. The crowd was clapping their hands demanding an encore. One minute passed, and another, before the statue came back to life.

"No encore!"

That would have been too much. The last of the stage lights faded off.

HUMANITY AU NATUREL

The family of Papparazzi's adult daughter was visiting London for the weekend. The family resided in an Airbnb flat in Southwark, since Papparazzi's pint-sized condo was too cramped to accommodate all of them. The foursome had arrived in the metropole late Friday evening, and Papparazzi went to collect his grandchildren, Nella and Eeli early in the Saturday morning in order to take them to London Zoo. Julia and her spouse Tuomas were planning to go downtown to do some shopping together. London was a familiar place to the parents, but for the children it was the first time. After purchasing tickets, Grandpa, Nella and Eeli headed straight to the Animal Adventure, which was a playground customised to the children. The time was flying as they were walking on the wobbly bridges, going down the slides and climbing up and down the ladders and the small climbing wall. They made imaginary trips around the world on the animal themed spring swings. The seaside trip with a catfish was the most memorable one. In the outdoor theatre they discovered exiting stories of llamas roaming through The Andes and the way of life meerkats led in the Kalahari Desert. Nevertheless, the most wonderful thing to Nella and Eeli was to get acquainted with the established residents of the corral, dwarf goats, mini-pigs, porcupines, mongooses and horned owls. At the same time, they acquired knowledge of all the creatures big and small in appropriate dosages. Spluttering in the aquapark crowned the adventure tour by providing cooling on the sun-drenched day.

After devouring fish and chips, the trio strode to the Bear Mountain where there was an exhibition rarity on display that weekend. The two towheads got wide-eyed seeing humans wearing only swimsuits and fig leaves instead of bears inside the fenced area.

"Why are there people hoofing around?"

Grandpa had done his homework, so he had his answer ready.

"The organisers of the expo wanted to make it clear that we humans are animals as well. We are primate mammals too."

The children were interestingly watching from the platform, how their conspecifics frolicked around the pasturage: played ball games, listened to music, took bites on bananas, sipped water and chattered with each other. Papparazzi picked up his camera from his bag and Nella and Eeli got their own mobile phones.

The Grandpa Gang was flamed up instantly. The shooting gave a new perspective on the capers. Their look was more detailed in a different way. Even one special face, stagger, a kiss on the cheek, giggle or incidence could turn out to make a lot of money. There were a lot of shooters around them. The only ones having no cameras were the ones inside the fenced area.

"I'm sure they have hidden their phones somewhere in the rock crevices ready to retrieve them, when nobody's watching from this side," Nella suspected. "Nobody can survive that long without them nowadays!"

Eeli accompanied his big sister asking immediately a question that had been preoccupying his mind after her comment.

"Where are their sleeping quarters?"

"Although they are treated the same as the other animals in the zoo, they are allowed to have one exception. In the evening they can go home. This way it's guaranteed they are bright and shining once they get back on the job in the morning."

"Oh, weak! The other animals would go on strike, if they knew what was going on!" Nella ejaculated.

Her witty comment made Papparazzi burst out with laughter.

When they had captured a hefty supply of images, they packed their gear and went on to explore other offerings the zoo was providing. The most interesting beasts, in the eyes of the kids, let them down by spending the hotness of the day in the shadowy quarters of their cages. In the late afternoon the parents announced having picked some great pieces from the shops and were missing the apples of their eyes to join them. Before granting their wish, the gang explored the day's captures inside pappy's Ford. He sent the advance ones from his laptop. Whether the news desks would get excited by them was anybody's guess. The subject had been featured prominently in the press, which made the trio's offerings less desirable. At this point no prospective buyers had emerged, but after they had scrutinised the whole lot, some deals could be coming their way. Before hitting the accelerator, Pappy chanted a jingle he had found from a newspaper. It was made by Brendan Carr – one of the residents in the Bear Mountain: "I'm funky like a monkey and as cool as a cat, talk more than a parrot, up all night like a bat. I got a laugh like a hyena but get the hump like a camel, so cover me in fig leaves as I'm the ultimate mammal."

Since the day in London had been an exciting one, both parties agreed to go their separate ways for the evening. On Sunday, well before the Tourunen family's return flight to Helsinki-Vantaa Airport was due, Papparazzi offered them a brunch at the Floral Room in Covent Garden. Edna joined in at the garden-like courtyard in order to introduce herself to her life partner's nearest kin.

"This kind of beauty, Edna Hill, I have found by my side to sweeten my life!" The lucky dog presented his muse.

The appropriate handshakes and hugs followed the announcement. Julia and Tuomas had brought the souvenirs they had purchased on the previous day. The mugs and the shirts with a Union Jack printing were scrutinised with care. They had also bought some tea. Edna received a Moominmamma and Papparazzi got a Moominpappa mug.

"These are our presents to you two. They contain also a little hint on these to both of you." Julia smiled contently.

"What would that be? We do have to find that out together, don't we?" Edna uttered.

When the main events of the Finnish-English love story were walked through, the most colourful tosses and turns were presented in a child-friendly way. So far, the cultural differences were almost non-existent in the couple's opinion.

The tabloid photographer's phone vibrated in the middle of forking his calamari dish. He couldn't help but to take a sneak peek at what the message he had received was all about. His expression lighted up. It was something he had to share with the others.

"You're not going to believe this! *Ellie* magazine is buying five photos of the whole kit. The best thing is that some of Eeli and Nella's takings are included in the deal. Now is the time for high-fives!"

The grandpa and kids slapped hands, cheered and toasted with glasses. Pappy promised to make sure that the children were duly compensated on the reward jackpot, which could be just nominal and also the printed version would be delivered in their home address as a memento. The eaters took their turns in admiring the shots *Ellie* had qualified for publishing. The masterpieces taken by the wee shooters took the main focus. In one of Eeli's captures the half-naked hominoids were grooming each other. Nella had been able to push through two pictures of relaxed people sunbathing.

"You children can be proud of yourselves! There's nothing you cannot do, if you go on with your hobby growing up. Who knows, maybe you will someday exceed your pappy's achievements!" Edna painted their future.

"Oh, yeah!" the siblings cried.

As the waiter of La Goccia was serving their desserts on the table, the scarf guy's phone came alive again. It was Graham.

"Hi, Papparazzi! Hope I'm not disturbing your weekend getaway badly, but there is something steaming up in London Zoo making me wish you could take a hike in there asap."

"What's the matter?"

"In the human farm, one of the couples is feeling amorous. Adam and Eve seem to have taken something stronger than water. It's touch-and-go whether they are already mating there. This is it, my dear friend! And the more of the dirty stuff, the merrier, please!"

After the phone call was cut off, the receiver announced he had got an urgent assignment to be handled immediately. He spared them from the gory details. The piece of news was annoying although they all knew he was working on a 24/7 attitude. The farewells ahead of plans were emotional. While Julia was hugging her dad, she said that their return flight would start off in three and a half hours. After their moment of delicacy, they would go back to their Airbnb condo and fetch their luggage before taking the underground from downtown to Heathrow Airport. For the camera guy time was of the essence. It was literally breathing down his neck as he saddled up his vehicle – Edna as his co-pilot – towards the latest adventure. God forbid, what was to be expected in Regent's Park!

SHOOTING STARS IN HEATHROW

British Airways and Heathrow Airport wanted to raise their image by calling *Grace*'s representatives to get an exclusive story. They had promised the subjects, the shooting stars, would be revealed just on the D-Day. The women's magazine had hired Papparazzi to shoot the pictures. He had arrived early to the airport, the event was due in an hour. He sat on the wall bench glancing through the international flights Terminal Two. Passengers of all shapes and sizes were flowing past him. The crew members stood out in their stylish, colourful uniforms. The roof structures resembled the wings of a plane with built-in-windows between them. On the glass wall above him there was a decorative propeller. His gaze was also attached to the steel columns within the lobby and the black partitions with yellow sideboards marked by capital letters A to D in order to guide the passengers to the right directions. The ribboned metal posts controlled the flow. People were packed around the check-in machines. Farther back officials assembled travellers' luggage. Eventually a luscious chick in her high heels strutted to Papparazzi and tapped his shoulder.

"Hi! You must be the Finnish photographer?"

Papparazzi sprang up and shook the hand of the female reporter introducing herself as Molly O'Brian. When given a chance, he enhanced the fact that there were two Ps between the As.

"A strange name you have thrown out on you. The priest

must have been wasted when baptizing you," she cracked.

The smiles enlightened both of their faces. While they were waiting for the inviters, they pondered what the shooting stars were all about. The answer was nowhere to be found, but when the airline's spokesperson Mildred Donovan joined in with them, the veil of secrecy parted a little. As it turned out, British Airways and Heathrow Airport had hired a star duo for two weeks to brighten their public image. One star worked as a passenger ambassador and the other as stewardess.

"They have worked undercover for the past week and are getting trained for their duties at the same time. From this day on they are working under their own names," Mildred explained.

The curious photographer and the reporter followed the secretive spokesperson, who led them into the space separating partitions A and B. Mildred let the tension rise unbearably high before revealing the true identity of the first celebrity.

"Just humour me a little longer! You'll recognise her the minute you lay your eyes on her."

At last, a group of suits miraculously showed up with Cheri Campbell, best known from her membership in the Piri Piri Girls pop band, dressed in a black skirt and purple T-shirt. The gentlemen belonged to the management team of the companies. The bosses introduced themselves and Cheri more thoroughly to Molly and Papparazzi. The red-haired female musician smiled benevolently to the appraisals. The nightingale carrying a pet name of Chili had kept her girl-next-door-look even in her forties. Although the sexy girl band had gone their separate ways, each of them still remained in the columns of gossip magazines. Chili summed up the idea of the PR-commission she had received with enthusiasm:

"Our main target is to ease the lives of the passengers."

The first week she had spent there dressed as an Indian lady had gone smoothly.

"It is wonderful to continue this work as myself. I'm eagerly waiting to see how people will react seeing me as a Passenger Ambassador."

The bosses left the invited guests to Mildred's caring hands to get on with their task. Once the Passenger Ambassador and the stewardess had been dealt with, they would be lunching together in the departure lounge. Molly started writing and Papparazzi went on with his shooting.

"The passengers have all kinds of questions, everything between Heaven and earth. We as ambassadors try to answer them to the best of our ability."

"What is the most common question in here?" Molly enquired.

The answer was spontaneous:

"Where should I go next? The questions of the airport services, timetables and check-in points are the never-ending subjects people ask."

Having a friendly attitude made all the difference. All the colleagues were eager to give assistance to a rookie like her in tricky situations.

The first customer turned to Chili. A Dutchman tall as a hob pole wanted to know where he could stuff himself. Cheri pointed at the Costa Café.

"That way, sir!" she chirped not being able to contain the legendary question: "Don't you know who I am?"

The beanpole froze on the spot stunned. Cheri let him out of his misery by revealing her secret.

"I thought I knew you from somewhere, but I couldn't put my finger on it. What a surprise!"

After Jouke de Vries from Haag received an autograph on the back of his hand from Chili, he grabbed her on the whirls of dance. Cheri cut the pirouettes short and commended her cavalier as a skilful dancer.

"Don't leave your day job just yet!"

The guy took off with chuckles towards the coffee shop. One or other passers-by recognised the superstar, who spread out her autographs at an increasing pace and posed in photos together. Once one of the Piri Piri Girls' female fans chirped out loud Chili's presence in the premises, she was sieged. The working conditions of Molly and Papparazzi were weakened into non-existent, although Mildred made an effort to squeeze them in by elbowing the fans further away. The trio threw in the towel, when the crowd started singing 'Gimme More Sex', which was the best-selling hit of the girl band. A piece of arcane trivia popped in Papparazzi's mind; Chili was also known to dye her lower hair with henna. This was totally useless information to Papparazzi, since there was a designated horticulturist tending her bush. His name was Stan.

After they had hiked for fifteen minutes, the communicators arrived at a British Airways aeroplane arranged just for them. The visitors coming through the pipeline were greeted with a jaw-dropping sight: Ben Almeida, the Brazilian human chameleon, who had recently undergone a sex reassignment surgery. He had changed his name to Barbara. Since she was suffering from a severe case of bacterial and virus phobia disorder, she only waved her hand to them. The stewardess was wearing a naval blue tailored suit and side cap decorated with a metallic wing pin. She had wrapped a blue-white-and-red scarf around her neck. Her breast was so bulgy that it seemed to be bursting out at any moment and her bottom was so full of filling that it would have made Kim Kardashian green with envy. The best thing after the commotion was that there was no-one else in the plane. This gave Molly and Papparazzi the room to get on with their work – especially as Mildred withdrew herself further away to twiddle her phone. In the first week Barbara had used a black wig and thick-rimmed glasses in order to hide her true identity.

"Despite that I got a few pinches on my bum. The integrity of the staff must be guaranteed at any point, but I do have to confess the attention felt quite nice, since I have changed my gender from male to a female only a short while ago. It remains to be seen, whether the guys can keep their hands to themselves on my next flight to Lisbon. I very much doubt it!"

Barbara had gone through a lot of plastic surgeries before her sex reassignment. Her nose, jaw, ears, cheekbones, eyelids, buttocks and tummy had been operated on. It would have been easier to make a list of her non-operated body parts. The request of becoming a stewardess had struck her with surprise. But as of now, she wouldn't have changed a second of it. The atmosphere in the workplace was positive and the colleagues were supportive.

"They keep telling me, how much more attractive I look in person than in the photos in social media. I am truly convinced that once my followers find out my last adventure, I'll become a more meaningful influencer than I was before."

The reporter asked, if the bombshell had thought of hearing some criticism of her actions in the matter.

"Of course I have, but I have decided to let it go in one ear and out of the other. I'm living the best time of my life not harming anyone. I'm sorry, if my outgoing lifestyle makes my critics angry. It's their problem, not mine!"

"What kind of new aspects have you found, while working

up in the blue sky?"

"My dynamic work challenges me professionally building up my entrepreneurship into new heights. There are always new interesting problems waiting to be solved. And this girl has dealt with everything with flying colours!"

Once Molly had done her part, Papparazzi entered to shoot the stewardess from every possible angle. When he had gotten enough frames for the story, they shifted to the departure lounge to get some lunch. Mildred led them up the stairs to The Perfectionists' Café. There were over a dozen people sitting around the big table. The stars and the invited guests were situated in the middle opposite each other giving Papparazzi a good view of the boarding gates on the lower floor. Turning his head to the right he had a clear vision of the planes taking off and landing on the airfield. Delicious aromas of the food were floating in the air. The small talk soared until it was cut off by the arrival of the friendly waitresses. They took the orders in a jiffy. According to staff recommendations, Papparazzi ended up having a Giuseppe pizza covered with different kinds of cheeses and spicy sausage. He washed it down with lager. The others including Molly ended up with similar portions of food. Due to Cheri's and Barbara's strict diet they both chose salads. While waiting for their food and drinks, Papparazzi's gaze followed the playing lights on a high pillar decorated with disks and metal spikes. It had been installed in the downstairs Caviar House & Prunier Seafood Bar. Behind the clever construction there were looming some deciduous creations. The art showed its power once again. He also paid attention to the waiters and waitresses buzzing around the tables laying the white tablecloths and the cutlery on them. Blunt pops of wine bottle corks expedited the oncoming service. The Manager of Heathrow Airport Eric

Pringle tinged his glass with his spoon at the end of the table. The murmur subsided and the focus was on him.

"Once again, I want to welcome you all, especially our fixed stars Chili and Barbara and the working couple from *Grace* magazine. With your assistance I believe we can spread the positive message to the public how important the work we do in the airports and in the planes is, day in, day out."

"You bet we do!" Barbara exclaimed.

The boss took a little break and cast a glimpse to Papparazzi.

"Don't you have a saying in Finland about everything happening in threes?"

The curly nodded in agreement.

"Consequently, we do have one ace up our sleeve... Please, step forward Top Chef Heston Blumenthal!"

The owner of The Perfectionists' Café miraculously showed up in front of the ensemble dressed as a waiter carrying pizza plates on both his hands. Seeing the third shooting star caused cries of exclamation and made their enthusiasm hit the roof. Heston was famous for being a rewarded trailblazer of the culinary world. On his numerous TV shows he had enhanced the home-cooking classics and fed the astronauts. Papparazzi's first encounter with the chef had been when he watched the MasterChef Australia cooking contest. The guru's conception of the eatable garden had carved its way deep in the memory lockers of his brains. Heston and the other waiters started to serve the dishes around the table. Papparazzi left his meaty plate to steam off to its place and grabbed his camera. He couldn't waste another second capturing Heston! Molly also gravitated towards him.

"Have you ever been caked?" the reporter asked.

"No, but once I attended a Halloween party with a slice of bacon stuck to my forehead. It looked like a scar."

"You have also consumed mice. How did they taste?"

"They tasted good after being well done! I haven't a clue, why us Westerners tend to limit our carnivorism only to the few chosen productive livestock. In other parts of the world the rodents are the greatest treat!"

"What is your opinion of people constantly taking photos of their food and drinks in the restaurants?"

"I resent it deeply. The food shouldn't be left to cool down like that at all. Why should anyone build that kind of barrier between the dishes and the shooters?"

"You heard the man, Papparazzi!"

But he was oblivious to their talking. He was focused on the star who urged him to return to his table.

"I'll be here until the end of the day, so you can take as many pictures of me as your heart desires."

"In for a penny, in for a pound!"

The best parts of the pizza were the succulent base and the back-kicking spices. Molly asked her sidekick to take a sneak peek backwards. There was a large painting on the wall breathing Heston's philosophy on food – there's nothing you can't do with it.

"Look at the marbled meat at the upper corner on the right. It might just be a red herring. On the hands of that experimenter, it will probably turn out to taste like cream and strawberries."

Right then Papparazzi decided to bring Edna along to dine in the food oasis. He made a note to Mildred about it, who said it could be arranged whenever it was convenient for them. The shooter gave her the thumbs up and got cracking again. The last captures of Heston had to be taken in haste in order to get the story covering a few spreads and the cover ready to be issued in the printed magazine in three days. Molly was also about to leave.

As the cameraman was returning back to the heart of London by tube, there was an earworm in his head. It was Jamppa Tuominen's, who was a singer from Oulu, hit song 'A Shooting Star'. Paps reorganised the lyrics – describing his feelings in a better way. "Today I saw Cheri, Barbara and Heston. Their bright sparkle dimmed the other stars. And I realised that there is a big flame of passion burning inside of them. The glow of the superstars is so bright and epic!"

As the train plunged inside a dark tunnel, he made his wish. He was the only one who knew what it was due to it being so tiny and frail – hiding it deep into his heart.

A FAREWELL TO THE HANGOVER!

Papparazzi was spending an evening in the company of all times in the window table of The Gallery Pub. He was having drinks with the vocalist Dirk Hooper, guitarists Ken Jennings and Donald Evans, and drummer Sidney Walsh of The Rocking Bones. The scarf guy rested his bum at the end of the table, Dirk and Ken had their backs turned away from the window opening up to Aylesford Street and Don and Sid sat opposite the front men of the band. The long-haired rock roosters were in showy suits, since they had taken part in the opening of the title store of the band in Carnaby Street. The event had raised a total commotion of the audience. The Swinging Street was once again on everyone's lips casting its shadows on the shopping meccas like Oxford Street and Regent Street. The tap house was also crowded with people wanting booze and autographs from the stars on the side. There were pictures taken together as well. Graham had been able to lure the foursome into a soiree in Pimlico with the help of his club connections in order to test a new magic spray, a hangover eliminator called the Clean Spirit. The substance was supposed to remove the sulphites and other toxic chemicals from the alcohol. No more headaches and nausea with vomiting even after the heaviest of benders ever. It sounded like a dream come true like the wish of all the lakes turning into liquor in a Finnish drinking song. Dirk had not hesitated at all, when the editor in chief had asked him to perform as a guinea pig in the trial. All the other members of the group showed little boyish enthusiasm to the experiment.

"Why hasn't anyone developed this before? We could have avoided a pile of hangovers over the years with a substance like this!"

The reporter of *London Star*, Melissa Lachey, had already chatted with the musicians. As she was with a family, her schedule didn't allow her to attend any extra-curricular activities. Their task was to get every musician to have one and the same kind of drink throughout the evening and write a report on their impressions. The assumption being they were all happy campers as they woke up. The shooter had dozens of small brightly coloured spray bottles as a gift for the trial from the product manufacturer in his bag, since he was in charge of the correct administration of the substance. Dirk had chosen Gin & Tonic for his poison tonight, Ken took whiskey, Don was a red wine man and Sid had chosen stout. In between spraying the substance and shooting photos the watchman poured lager down his throat. He was participating in the experiment just for fun. The sensational magazine had left the tab open.

The star visit meant the world to The Gallery Pub. When the landlady Wilona had heard of the visit just before the D-Day, she had jumped for joy before ordering some extra staff to serve the celebs.

"Oh, Pappy, you are a miracle worker! This night will make a great chapter in our pub chronicles with capital letters!"

Papparazzi had downplayed his part of the deal giving the honours to Graham Stone and his accomplished network.

"But without you they would be boozing somewhere else!"

The Finn had to agree that it was the truth.

Once the drinking roulette had started spinning, the waiters asked the persons present give the research workers the space to do their jobs. The request was complied meticulously albeit the eyes glued to the testers. Dirk's glass got five sprays, Ken's got seven, Don's three and Sid's got eight. He spiced his own drink even more thoroughly with twenty sprays. He wasn't going to be the one having the after effects of this bacchanalia! The sides of the glasses hit each other whereafter they wet their windpipes. Papparazzi raised his camera instead of his glass. The first reaction was positive – none of the scientists reported having an under-taste as the flashlight went on. After multiple drinks and sprays the atmosphere started loosening up. It encouraged Papparazzi to inquire about the amounts of women they had made out with.

"Warren Beatty boasted of sleeping with thirteen thousand women. The reporter never figured out to ask, if the right number was twelve thousand nine hundred ninety-nine. You are free to calculate our score numbers based on that," the vocalist chuckled.

The old fellas admitted generously that the dalliance was being more inactive by now.

"Especially since drinking and tittle-tattling on a man-to-man basis makes romances unlikely," Ken suspected.

"Don't give up yet! The evening is so young. Knowing you – and your history – there might be a chance for you to pick up a pub rose to keep you warm!" Sid encouraged.

Pappy told how someone made a sudden pass at him recently.

"I was returning home from a shooting gig feeling exhausted until a neon-sign with Sauna written on it jumped out in front of my eyes in Vauxhall. Us Finns are the hardest sauna-bathers in the world so I decided to blow my cobwebs away in there.

Subsequently I realised seeing only a part of the sign due to the burnt lamps, but I will explain that later. I hadn't been in a sauna for months – as a Finn I couldn't resist the temptation. After parking my car, I stepped into the world of steam."

The primeval rockers had focused their ears and eyes on him. Ken's sticky-ears were almost flapping as he was waiting for the continuation of the tale with great interest.

"I took all my clothes off as it is customary in my country and covered my jingles with a tiny towel. There were many offers of back rubs and free drinks coming my way. Later on, I comprehended being the new guy on the block among the regulars…"

Don threw in a question:

"And all the participants were male, I gather?"

"Exactly! I realised a little too late where I had stuck my nose and weenie. I know now better than well that homosexuality flourishes above all in London saunas!"

"Well, what happened next?" Dirk pried.

"A certain hairy-ass didn't seem to keep his hands to himself although I kept telling him I wasn't interested. Once his dick began to come in to life, I hauled my ass out of the steam room and made my escape just flipping my clothes on! The rest of the journey was sweaty, since I hadn't had time to shower due to the commotion in there."

Wilona and her helpers filled their glasses at the same pace as they emptied them. Papparazzi took his story to the finale with froth from the lager on his upper lip.

"There is one thing I learned from my jump to the unknown. Whenever I feel like getting into the steam, I'll be rushing to the Finnish Seamen's Mission. That sauna cleanses both my body and soul. If I ever get to go into a place like Naughty Men's

Sauna, there will be a pair of words tattooed on my buttocks: Exit Only!"

Once they had picked up the speed, the members of The Rocking Bones had a memory or two to share. Sidney got down the memory lane first.

"When we were just a rising band, we used an open top double-decker on our tours. I remember lively, how we used to tan ourselves in the midst of bare-breasted chicks on the top floor. We boozed, smoked pot and made love all day long."

They all confirmed the recollection to be true. The country folks in particular despised their way of life. Getting rich was the most unforgettable thing for Donald.

"Personally, the culmination point of my buying sprees was when I ordered pizza from New York to London… as a take-away. It was good and I ate it all but don't ask what it cost. I have no desire of knowing."

"It cost you an arm and a leg at any rate!" Ken added charging after his own memory imprint.

"In our first American tour we resided in the hotels of the same chain. I have no desire to repeat the name in this context. Having taken our heads full of speed we threw out the TVs, furniture and cocktail trays – the glasses were full of the most expensive mixed drinks – down the hotel room windows to the streets, wiped the place with mustard, ketchup and mayonnaise and broke the sinks leaving water running. Well, it was so stupid!"

"But fun though!" Ken assured.

The hotel chain had taken its time to cut a lot of slack to their Teutonic romping until they had banned the whole band for life from their hotels. The police had been involved as well.

"We are not up to any mishaps any more. Being an elderly

gentleman obliges distinguished behaviour," the number one guitarist finished his part of the tale.

All of them turned their attention to Dirk. What kind of highlight would he be revealing?

"I was sitting in an underground train in the 1970s, minding my own business, believe it or not. Of course, I took an effort to be as unnoticed as possible, having even raised my jacket collar upright. At Camden Town station in comes a long-haired man with his guitar. Playing in the train was a rare thing even then. The street musicians were treated as a nuisance and pickpockets. The travellers grabbed their purses and bags when seeing the shady guy. His artistic effort was expected to be horrendous."

Dirk took a little pause licking his lips.

"The hippie started to strum our hit song '(I Can't) Get It Up'. Dangdang-dang-dang-dangly-dang… The listeners became vigilant. The bums started to wiggle on the seats, the fingers drummed the armrests and soon the whole carriage, me among the others – repeated the lyrics: 'I Can't Get It Up! Without You!' Some of them jumped up and danced wildly. The street musician's collecting box and pockets were filled with coins and notes."

Based on the sensitive feelings surrounding the table his story had hit the mark. In the end Don broke the silence with tears in his eyes:

"That's an awesome story! It touched the bottom of my heart. We have done something right along the way!"

The men toasted to that. Did they have an umpteenth number of drinks going down? Nobody could remember. Papparazzi had also forgotten to do his magic. He handed over the spray bottles and urged them to follow their conscience, when spraying the substance in. Sid was counteracting his hangover heavy-handedly adding the whole bottle to his drink.

Just before closing time Wilona came to announce the party was about to end soon. That was all it was about, since the whole pub full of people were buzzing around the stars. Hugs, praises, intimate taps on the shoulders, autographs, mobile phone pictures, cheerfulness... All of that was spinning inside Papparazzi's head like a spinning-top. He must be really drunk! He had to get some fresh air outside at any cost... The rockers were also following the cameraman's example, since they were struggling to get rid of all the people wanting to get their attention. The wild fivesome established science having taken a giant leap ahead. However, they were staggering a lot as they were bidding longing farewells. Possessing a knowledge of no hangover looming in a few hours empowered the boozers, when they were scattered in the different sides of the metropole.

Papparazzi woke up at ten in the morning with a rigorous hangover. This should not have happened here. First he rushed to his toilet seat to throw up and then to the medicine cabinet in order to hoard some painkillers. Had this happened also to the other scientists? He had received a text message from Melissa. She was wondering why she hadn't received any written reports from the rays of sunshine. The reporter had started phoning around, since her story was due by the end of the evening. Papparazzi notified in his answer that he was about to be sending the photos in a jiffy. They would be at her disposal in an hour, tops.

In the afternoon Papparazzi received a summary of the experiment, when Melissa called him.

"Are you sitting down firmly at home?"

"Yes, on my porcelain throne in the loo... This day has gone down the drain for sure, I'm still feeling quite wobbly."

"You are not alone in this! Don is bedridden and scorching in the flames of hell. He told me that with a hoar sounding like his voice was coming beyond the grave so your depiction is correct. Dirk had woken up early in order to go on his morning jog, but before that he had been forced to swallow a handful of painkillers and vitamins just to get rid of his pains and cramps. Sid had collapsed on his living room floor and is still lying in there according to his wife – vomit still dangling on his lips. Ken is also at death's door. He was just mumbling on his phone that Montezuma's revenge is alive... Then he was cut off."

"So, we've all been had big time! Clean Spirit is just a hoax!"

"This is the basis of my story. The whole Kingdom gets to hear the incorruptible truth!"

"Go for it!"

In the evening Papparazzi felt better. He scrutinised the writing on the package of Clean Spirit. With the smallest possible print – on the last row – there was a following statement:

"The best way of avoiding the hangover is to stop drinking alcohol."

After he had assimilated the fact, only one question came to his mind: Is annoyance lethal?

BLIND DATE WITH BANKSY

Edna and Papparazzi were having coffee in the Draughts Board Game Café on Leake Street. The table was just outside the café in the Banksy Tunnel giving them plenty to feast their eyes on in the form of street art on offer.

"All credit and honour to Tate Britain, Tate Modern and the National Gallery, but if you ever want to get a sense of the hottest trends in art, this is the place to be," Edna emphasized.

She visited the shrine of the street regularly in order to suck in some fresh breezes. It was essential to a gallerist to see what was going on in time. The visitations had an impact on her choosing, which artist and what kind of artwork she wanted to display in the Snow White Gallery. Papparazzi had joined her in order to photograph some of the creations. This way she could make comparisons between the older and newer works whenever she felt like it. One of the appealing features of the tunnel was the periodical change in the paintings displayed on the walls. Although Banksy had made it all happen, having held the Can Festival on these premises, none of his works were not seen or admired by friends of graffiti art. Edna also made a blockbuster revelation:

"Banksy is aware of us two being in here today! I sent him a text message on this subject. He gave me a thumbs up."

Papparazzi almost fell off his chair as adrenalin was bursting through his veins since he had made the acquaintance of the famous street artist both in Helsinki and in London. He was certain of having caught a glimpse of him. Though he had failed to recognise him or capture his image on film. No-one had been able to take his mask off. His identity was still a total enigma. Or should we say them, a group of artists? The Finn's senses steeled up. Could he make the reveal of a lifetime with his shooting equipment? Although the money was only a footnote in capturing the giant kahuna, this kind of photo could make Papparazzi a filthy rich man.

"That's why I contacted Banksy. He just might seize the opportunity." Edna added fuel to a fire. "The two of you have so much in common. Danger attracts you both. Only amateurs and bedwetters ask permission!"

They both burst out with laughter that seemed to last forever. Eventually as they were able to put their act together at least somehow, there was time to focus on the immediate surroundings. Basically every space available had been utilised for creativity. Beside the door of the board game café was an abstract HAM artwork, its pink and orange colouring jumped into one's eyes and stylized letters were scattered partly on top of each other. In the middle there was the peace symbol. Opposite the entrance of the café there was a concrete pillar with a pair of affectionate puffins painted on it.

"Those two seem as happy as we are!" Papparazzi noted as he was raising his camera.

Near the pillar there was a leprechaun keeping guard, pointing out that if you don't behave yourselves, he might get nasty. But if and when you are favourable, he can lead you to the treasure hidden under the will-o'-the-wisp.

"That guy breathes the Irish folklore. On the green moors of Ireland there are the oddest creatures lurking around, if you know where to look. And one of the strangest characters has made its way here," Edna cracked.

They got up off the table and made their way towards The Vaults venue. On the way they paused to admire a large ceiling painting by Olivierr, where a young long-haired blond was focusing on her mobile phone. A tight sweater caressed her figure. The lights were changing colours in disco-style from blue to lilac and white to red.

"Olivierr is a talented and well-beloved artist. He can paint abstract as well as beautiful female faces. His murals have conquered the world," Edna introduced.

The masterpiece pleased Papparazzi's eyes too. The deeper look he cast on it, the more it pleased him. At The Vaults their attention was caught by a monochrome painting resembling Picasso's style and an environmentally themed mural painted to imitate a brick wall with different kinds of sea creatures. "An irresponsible human sows destruction around him." A painting featuring a mad scientist with a crazy gloss in the eyes through his blue-tinted specs, quite similar to those worn by Finnish entertainer Mikko Alatalo as his trade mark, conducting a lobotomy to a naked male. The poor exploited fellow was assured – as his brain mass was coming out of his skull, some of it stashed in a jar – that he was in good hands, safe...

Edna and Papparazzi had also paid attention to other people passing them by with scrutiny. No-one looking like Banksy had crossed their path. Until Edna's gaze caught a man in black, his hood pulled over the head, a bag at his feet. He was busy with his spray paint cans. The gallerist grabbed Papparazzi's arm without uttering a word and nodded towards Bob the Builder. The scarf guy got it in a jiffy what she was after. He asked Edna to take care of his gear in a subdued voice and sprinted off. The echo of his footsteps didn't go unnoticed by his adversary. He got startled, grabbed his play bag and started off towards the exit.

"Hi, Banksy! Stop!"

As Papparazzi was capturing the runaway, he was pushed from the back. Edna's warning cry about Banksy's helper was too late in catching his ears and he tripped on his feet. He fell on the ground headlong trying to shelter his camera with both hands. The male duo got out scot-free, turning left on the tunnel exit. Papparazzi caught a glimpse of Banksy's face. He would never forget the covered up face with a scarf up to his nose, dark eyebrows and pilot glasses.

Edna rushed to help the fallen high speeder get back on his feet.

"Are you sure you're okay?"

"I think I'll live through a few more skin scratches."

Edna examined the victim's ribs for fractures, but he was not in excruciating pain. His breathing was effortless. He was adamant about not requiring any medical help, which was well received by his honeyed lady. She wouldn't have done it either.

"The handyman was keeping guard near Banksy, pretending to watch the art on the wall. In fact, he followed Banksy's working out of the corner of his eye incessantly and rushed on his way like a coppertop, when the situation came on. I'm tremendously upset at not warning you off in time."

"It should have occurred to me as well that he might have brought an accomplice with him. The most annoying thing for me was that I was in such close proximity to the greatness and not getting a picture of him!"

Edna caressed her sweetie's blonde hair.

"Well, we can't help it now... Nevertheless, Banksy was camouflaged so well, nobody could have identified him from the photo anyway."

"It is a cold comfort for me – I'll never get to check out the big bucks over this."

Once the sorrows and troubles had been dealt with, they went to the painting Banksy had left behind. It represented an angry young man with writing on his T-shirt: "Beat it! We've been had!" The youngster held a flag in his hand claiming: "We want answers!" Banksy's signature was featured in the bottom. Edna elbowed Papparazzi on the side and started to see light at the end of a tunnel.

"You'll get to take pictures of Banksy's newest creation!"

The scarf guy's eyes brightened up.

"Edna, you are an angel! Of course! They will be easily sold. How on earth did I never think about that?"

"Well. It is a well-known fact that us women can multitask several things simultaneously opposed to you men's one-track way of thinking."

Papparazzi didn't start arguing. He set his camera to sing odes to the mural instead.

When walking on the Lower Marsh hand in hand, they decided to indulge themselves by having a glass of wine. The Vaulty Towers pub was a colourful place on the outside, making it impossible to pass by when you wanted to quench your thirst. The interior turned out to be artistic as well – a good continuation of Leake Street. They were already all liquored up, when Edna got a message from Banksy.

"Hello again, Edna and Papparazzi! Once I found what you two were planning to do today, I felt shit for not having a piece of my own art in my tunnel. I had to make things right. I had no intention to work while you two were in the premises. It just happened. After you caught up with me, I was making the last strokes on my *Street Fighting Man* painting. It is something you can and should be shooting, Papparazzi! My assistant is truly sorry for doing what he did to you in order to protect me. He sends his apologies. I hope you weren't hurt in the action. I wish you to understand that my true identity must stay secret. Or am I a group of artists? I fully comprehend that many people would like to unmask me and make a fortune out of it. You didn't make it today, Papparazzi, although I have to admit in all honesty it was a close call. No hard feelings on our blind date, do you agree? Best wishes, Banksy."

In their answer to him they assured him everything was all right including the apologies, the medication, photos of the painting and relationships. The surprise date was something they would remember with warmth. If Banksy would ever be rethinking and being prepared to make the biggest revelation of the century, i.e. to come forward with his true name and identity, he knew that he could call Papparazzi at any time.

DEATH ON THE THAMES

Papparazzi was lurking beside *The Battle of Britain* monument at Victoria Embankment. The star soprano Tara Liebermann had been spotted jogging there several nights prior. The cameraman spent several nights in there but struck out every time. He wasn't expecting to bring home the bacon since Tara's career was on the downward slide. She was best known by the masses for her duet 'The Night Shining Clouds' with an Italian tenor Amadeo Vasari. Pedestrians and runners passed by. Papparazzi raised the binoculars he had brought along with his long objective camera to his eyes. He got alerted seeing a brunette familiar to the public jogging towards him. The runner had just passed *The Royal Air Force Memorial*. The shooter hadn't a second to spare. The photographer focused his camera on the subject from his station and started shooting on automatic fire. With a brisk swap to a smaller objective and a step forward from the sight-screen, he went on intensely. Tara didn't let Papparazzi disturb her zen-like state. Her gaze was focused aside on the River Thames.

"Tara, you're a star! Can you take a look here!"

The singer lost her cool for a moment and a smile swept over her face. Better still, she did what she was told, the scarf guy felt he was hitting a bullseye with his fingertips.

"Thanks! You are cracking gorgeous!"

The Velvety Pipes went on her way, leaving only a rosy scent of her lingering in the air. It faded quickly. He heard somebody calling his name behind him. The male voice was distinctly familiar to him, but Papparazzi couldn't tell offhand, who the short-winded bloke approaching him was.

"Papparazzi! What a coincidence!"

As a smallish man with dark eyes took a hold of Papparazzi's sleeve, he realised with whom he had the honour to discuss: The most notorious actor of Hercule Poirot, Sir David Suchet! The Finn almost crapped his pants.

"I happened to be here in order to take shots, mostly of the landscapes, myself as well, when I spotted you working! I don't know, if I did the right thing or not, but I captured your encounter with Tara from the side. They came out splendidly, I can assure you!"

"Where do you know me from?"

"I have read your undertakings from the papers. You made a great entrance to London!"

Well, of course he had, Papparazzi thought to himself as he was pinching himself once more in order to believe the grand old theatre actor accompanying him. Introductions on both sides sealed the fact. There was no sign of Hercule Poirot's well-arranged dress, David Suchet's attire looked rather shabby. The fact that photography had been his hobby for decades came out quickly.

"What's up with us colleagues, right?"

The comment was followed by a hearty hug. The Poirot actor was not as chubby in real life as he was in the TV series, followed by hundreds of millions of viewers all around the globe. He took his adversary's hand leading him to sit on the nearest bench. This time he didn't underlay his handkerchief before sitting.

"We do have a lot to talk about." He made an educated guess.

At first, they sat quietly letting their gazes sweep over the Thames. Riverboats went up and down. On the opposite shore the London Eye spun its slow cycle like a giant bagel. Car honking blended with the hustle and bustle of the city. David showed his exposures from the screen of his camera. They were so revealing that Papparazzi made an immediate order to get them into his home album. The actor was fine with it. He didn't want any monetary compensation as he took them purely for his own pleasure. Papparazzi wanted also to take some photos of his camera-buddy. He generously admitted his intention of selling them. His pal was favourable to this. The Finn rolled up his sleeves immediately. In most shots David had his shooting gear prominently displayed. The other walkers let them hustle in peace so they were able to finish in a quarter of an hour. At last, the flood gates of the words opened. Papparazzi chose willingly to listen – the moment at hand was so exceptional.

"I consider myself a painter, the camera is my brush. London is an endless spring of inspiration for me. Objects, people, buildings, parks, water features et cetera make me sparkle. Post boxes of the Victorian Era, the red phone boxes and double-deckers ignite my flame."

In his opinion the best lens was your own eye. He found the game of light and shadow especially enchanting. Changing the angle, for example a shot taken under another person's arm, the most extraordinary things can take on a new artistic dimension. The plays were also like pictures. Small display windows of our world.

Papparazzi signed his intelligent characterisations as such. They qualified as well in his line of work, even though it was marked with a special stamp of commercialism. The subject matter was also specified: the celebrities. The paparazzi photos told a tale of our society and the world us humans live in. They were important platforms – art – of our time. Whatever else could they have been?

A slowly strutting spinster broke the bubble they had formed around them, as after some thought and pondering, she encouraged herself to gravitate to the men.

"Is it Mr Poirot himself sitting in there? Has there been a murder around here?" the round-spectacled auntie enquired.

She was intrigued with a smile on her face, while she was listening to the world-famous detective's answer.

"Not at all, madame. I'm quite confident that nothing of the sort will take place, not nearby at any rate."

"What brought you here then?"

"Me and my photographer friend are just making the world a better place!"

"Well, that's nice. Enjoy your evening, both of you."

"And you too. And as you know, milady, when I'm around you can proceed to your destination safe and sound! When the perps see me hanging around, they abandon their evil deeds immediately due to the fact I'll be on their track with certainty."

"Oh, thank you! Thank you for protecting me!"

When she had gained some distance away from them, Papparazzi wondered how and why on earth she had confused David Suchet with Hercule Poirot? While photographing he was the opposite of the latter.

"Once in a while, although it is rare, things like this come my way, i.e. I'm addressed as Hercule Poirot, while I'm as much as myself as I ever could be. Some people are dead serious, some try to be funny. That's why I take all the approaches so matter-of-factly."

He was recognised as Poirot by his eyes, voice and the shape of his skull, sometimes from the back of his head. He found these encounters enchanting.

"They are big contributions to my work as an actor."

What was the secret of the main character Agatha Christie had written? David had no comprehensive answer to this question, but he brought up some positive facts of the character he played.

"Although Hercule Poirot is pompous and his ego has swollen in gigantic proportions, he always addresses people politely – even the servants. He takes good manners for granted. In his famous closing speech, he can flip his lip and believe the culprit will deserve a punishment on their evil deeds, but doesn't take away their dignity. The biggest reason for his popularity is that he is always on the good and right side of things. He wants to expose and hold accountable those who harm other people."

Poirot's solitude got him a lot of sympathy. His need of love in his life was something everyone could relate to. Although he solved crime cases masterfully, the mystery of love remained unsolved.

There were no bloodbaths in Agatha Christie's novels – the victims were killed rarely with firearms or edged weapons. Poisoning was the most common choice for murder. David provided his knowledge of the poisons used as quick as a shot – neat and secure means of killing: arsenic in *4.50 From Paddington*, strophanthin in *Triangle at Rhodes*, taxine in *Pocketful of Rye*, snake venom in *Murder in The Clouds* and nicotine in *Three Act Tragedy*.

"The victims consumed them in their food or drink. Speaking of them, I have coffee as a picnic beverage. Would you like some? Of course you would, you're a Finn. I have read that you people are the biggest coffee consumers per capita," David said and grabbed a thermos from his camera bag. "This keeps the coffee at drinking temperature for around twenty-four hours."

Papparazzi took on the offer with enthusiasm, confessing his coffee addiction. When receiving the thermo cup he leered at it.

"Oh, no my dear colleague! There is no poison in it. Have no fear of drinking it."

After a few gulps at the mug his grip loosened and it fell on the slabs spreading coffee on the ground. He gasped, his throat rattled and his limbs convulsed wildly. The scarf guy swayed on his seat falling on the ground face down. His hands had no strength left to cover it. He felt the taste of blood in his mouth meeting the hard ground and also a great desire to close his eyes and fall into everlasting sleep. David took a two-hand grip on the armpits of the drooping man and pulled him back to the seat.

"What a performance! You put your heart and soul into your part of a poisoned victim. The world has lost a great actor in you, Papparazzi!"

The grumbler returned from his state in a flick of a finger expressing his contentment after having been praised for his actions.

"I amazed myself with my performance as well! Did you have any doubt in your mind that I was at death's door?"

"Not more than a nanosecond, since I was well aware of the situation. Now we have to trust and believe that no harm took place in your little show."

"Trust me, I'm healthy as a horse. My belly flop looked worse than it was in reality – it was cat soft."

David was relieved at hearing this. Even as he captured a tip of an important notion he wanted to share with his colleague.

"Life's a play. We all put on our costumes every day according to where we work and who we meet. That's why it's so important that we pick the right role with care."

"Tell me about it!"

The artist nailed his dark eyes to the blond Viking until he broke the ice by prying:

"More coffee, sir?"

THE BAR-HOPPING PLAYBOY

The most famous rap artist Kevin East had flown across the big pond to London. After experiencing a religious revival, the musician wanted to expand his parish activities outside the States. His curvy spouse Zoe Castaneda had stayed put in New York. The hip-hopper's visit had remained under the media radar so far. A tip to *London Star* changed everything; the rapper's rented Fisker Karma was parked in front of the Corinthia Hotel on Whitehall Street. At nine p.m., the Duo Ramshackle arrived on the spot getting a visual of the luxury car. Rob parked his BMW X6 near the sand-coloured hybrid. The smash hits of the superstar had been shaking on their eardrums during the drive. Currently they were listening to a song called 'Bolder', which lyrics oozed sex: "Baby, will you be my – your boss's – naughty secretary tonight…"

"The most enthusiastic fans wish this to be the new national anthem of the United States, if he is becoming their new president," Rob explained.

"It might take some time still. Maybe he will gain more support in the coming presidential election," Papparazzi suspected.

"It remains to be seen. However, I know that if he had taken Zoe with him, the couple would have been bathing in the flashlights since the beginning. They wouldn't get a moment's peace before their return home," Rob mentioned.

"This is Kevin's second day here. It's astonishing how none

of the media have got on the story – yet. Graham promised us huge payoffs, if and when the newspaper will be the first in revealing the star visit with our help," Papparazzi enthused.

The significant challenge sharpened their senses. They glanced furtively around to see if there were more paparazzi around. It didn't appear to be the case. While one of Kevin's newest hit songs, 'Walkin' On Water', was playing, the chums contemplated the star's latest escapade: walking on water as a part of his Sunday Service ceremonies in Atlanta. The trick was performed by hiding a see-through platform just a couple of centimetres below the pond's surface. Some people still believed that the miracle had really happened.

"In any case think of the sex bomb Kevin is married to. Millions of men can only dream of the sweet rides he's getting in bed day in, day out," Rob pondered.

"Tell me about it! The rich lucky bastard is hiding somewhere inside that hotel," Pappy agreed.

The hotel entrance flew open, and a black male trio in their fashionable attire strode out. Kevin was among them. Papparazzi was crucially late on getting his camera up – when it was properly focused, the Fisker Karma had swallowed the trio inside. It pulled Rob off on their tail. The show was on! In the blink of an eye, they were going down Northumberland Avenue in a row and straightening up the traffic circle on Charing Cross. The pace was very fast with risky passes accompanied by endless hooting of the other cars. At Piccadilly Circus the lights turned red at the worst possible moment. They lost their target, when it cannonballed through the crossing. Rob was furious. His heavy left foot hit the engine room in rage. In Shaftesbury Avenue they caught up with the Fisker again.

A tight turn to the left on Dean Street and a sudden stop in the purple-lit front of the Sunset Strip club. Kevin and a colossal bloke, probably a bodyguard, entered the erotic oasis, while the hybrid took off. The camera objective dangled miserably on Papparazzi's neck. The likelihood of getting photos of the superhero was reduced.

"I never stood a fighting chance of getting to shoot Kevin. I just cannot keep up the pace."

Rob nodded as a sign of consent and reminded him the evening was young.

"It's not a lost cause yet. My car is now on tow-away so I have to find a parking spot for it first."

"I got you, boss! I'll step out and hang out to watch. We'll draw up a more detailed action plan, when you come back."

Soon the divergent rear lights of the BMW were the only visible sign of the car. The more Papparazzi contemplated the matter, the fleshier it started to appear. An international entertainer had just emerged inside the strip club to have some fun, while his wife Zoe was tending their young children somewhere else. Marital relationships had been put to the test for less in the past. Should they hem Kevin in, giving both of the Duo Ramshackle an equal chance of getting their own shots of the naughty boy – one in the inside and the other outside? Rob returned quickly and was warmed by the bold idea. He had only brought his mobile phone with him, since he had been rushed to the scene in the middle of his busy delivering schedule. It made him the best candidate to dive into the lion's den. After all he was a frisky bachelor looking for a good time.

"Should I get revealing photos, you can put your name on them as long as we share the profits."

They shook hands on it. The Finn felt warm and fussy seeing the black-haired guy was going through below the raised up-and-over garage door. This if anything was a bromance – a friendship at its purest form. No matter what the outcome was in this bold venture, he made his mind up on the spot to treat Rob to a night out with no limits in a beer house.

The waiting game was over when Kevin's assistant, a terrible bound of muscles, threw Rob out with a neck-ass-grasp down on the street. Papparazzi stepped right in to check on his companion's physical condition. He assured him that he was fine.

"All I got was some road rash. Time heals all of it."

"What on earth happened to you in there? You spent an eternity there before your flamboyant send-off."

"I started off with buying some soda and pushed myself to sit as near as I could get to Kevin at the showroom. It wasn't an easy task due to the place being so packed. He was left pretty much to himself. Either he was not identified in that kind of environment or the partygoers just wanted to respect his privacy. The climax came when one of the pole-dancers pulled a really dirty set and Kevin rushed on the stage, pushing a stash of cash down to her bra and panties. As a return he got a wild lap dance. I realised that was my cue and got my phone up into a shooting position. At the same moment I felt a peel-sized hand grabbing my neck and trouser collar. I insisted to the Gorilla – that was the most appropriate name I could come up with – that I was only taking some selfies. I also shouted out bloody murder. King Kong and the guards arriving to assist him never listened to my racket. They just claimed to be protecting the privacy of their high-priority guest. According to the security guards, it was a great honour when a Yankee greatness chose the Sunset Strip over all the erotic bars in London. The rest is history!"

"Oh, blimey, what a story!"

"You can say that again! The sadder side of it was that I

didn't get any pictures. I'm truly sorry!"

"It wasn't your fault! Higher powers than you intervened. In what kind of party mood is Kevin tonight?"

"He's been drinking like a fish in the bar. Unless he is the wonder man he claims to be, he must be wasted by now."

They agreed on the fact that Rob would retreat favourably to the side. He would stick out like a sore thumb to the Gorilla and the others raising their suspicions and making the alarms go off. That was something the daredevils couldn't afford. Besides, the erotic oasis was near its closing time. The men were rushing out of the sinful place at a growing pace. Papparazzi chose the front of the De Lane Tea studio across the street as his station. Just when he had set his camera steadily in his hands, Kevin staggered towards the door having a half-naked hottie on his tail. Out of the corner of his eye the shooter saw a familiar sand-coloured vehicle approaching the same spot. The finger hit the trigger the first time. And the second and the third. The flashes of the flash made the Gorilla behind the celeb and the stripper turn into a speed-runner in a fraction of a second hiding his boss from the shooter's vision in a jiffy. The Fisker Karma curved and parked in front of Papparazzi in order to screen his targets out of sight. He darted towards the car with his camera. The keystrokes were spastic. He heard the car door opening and saw Gorilla and Kevin diving on the backseat. The windows were tinted making the shooter try getting around the obstacle. After the door was closed, the driver stepped on the accelerator so hard that the front wheel almost rolled over the photographer's foot. Rob rushed to help his friend.

"That driver was trying to run you over!"

"My pantlegs are still shaking but fortunately that was all."

"Such a reckless driver should lose his licence over this!"

When they were able to catch their breath, the duo checked

the captured takings. As Rob had risen to the occasion a second too late, all he could offer was some more or less blurry photos. The rapper was nowhere to be seen in the middle of the mist.

"These ones can be deleted."

The tension rose to its peak when Papparazzi produced his picture screen. A few hits made him sigh in relief.

"Those first frames seem especially promising but later on they turn into a blurred mush," Rob estimated.

"It is as simple as that. I'll check them all when I get home. I have a nagging feeling of not getting any sleep tonight."

"Me neither, if I had such sensational material in my possession."

Using his home computer proved his presumption right. The fivesome in the beginning satisfied the most demanding eye – the imprints were razor-sharp. All of them were elevations on the doorway. The name of Sunset Strip was fully visible on top of Kevin and the half-naked kitty groping him. Papparazzi deduced that the latter had gotten a reward for her performance to last a lifetime and was rushing out in order to thank him. Notes were falling out of her thong on the doormat. The biggest difference with the photos was that in the first one her bare breast was visibly hanging out and in the fifth she was hiding behind the Gorilla. The more Papparazzi rolled the pictures on the screen, the more convinced he was that the first one hit the jackpot. He would process the picture with care before sending it. At six in the morning all of the sensational material was at the disposal of Graham and the editorial team. In an hour there was a story on the front page of *London Star* with an exclusive stamp on it. The chief editor was so happy with the global interest in the scoop that he was willing to add one more zero to the duo's reward. At midday the amount increased further. The Finn also got an unforgettable message from the leader of the publication: "I'm now announcing on behalf of our media company and the whole corporation that you have been rewarded with the Papparazzi Pulitzer!"

The commotion culminated, when Zoe made a statement by the end of the rock-hard news day. The queen of the jet set roasted her husband totally. He was supposed to be on a spiritual trip to London instead of being a bar-hopping playboy. The most shocking thing for her was that she had stayed home taking care of the children. In order to salvage their marriage they would need long-term therapy and other services from the shrinks. There would be an unforgettable welcoming party waiting for the returning hero.

A HYMN TO STREET URCHINS

According to Papparazzi's trusted source, Elaine – a pop singer with a dazzling career – was going to visit the legendary The Notting Hill Bookshop with her newest boyfriend Texaa. This was the first time ever anyone had a chance to capture the rapper and the popper together so the scarf guy hurried up to the scene. The beauty had recently broken up with her long-term life partner Norris Huber. Notting Hill was famous for the film carrying the same name, starring Julia Roberts and Hugh Grant. It was Elaine's favourite movie as well as her beloved residential area. The first time she had moved there just after coming of age, on the eve of her breakthrough.

Papparazzi was expecting Elaine and Texaa to arrive in front of the small large bookstore on the Blenheim Crescent. It had the spirit of the past time charm with red-brick-coloured columns framing its windows and doors. The shop's name glowed with gold letters on a blue base at the top of the shop window. He listened the megastar's hottest hits from his mobile phone. 'Burning Bush After Rain', 'Hitting The Bottom', 'Earthquake' and 'Fly Around in Circles' got him in a great mood. Elaine's tone of voice with its colours of blues and soul touched the innermost corners of the heart. Her interpretations were full of fire and water. The whole way up he had played Texaa's rhythms. 'Ibiza Forever', 'Unique Guy' and 'I'm Yours' were Papparazzi's favourite tunes. Since the lovebirds were nowhere to be seen, he transferred to Mike's Café across the street in order to slurp some mocha. It was good to keep waiting on the café terrace under the sunshade.

Papparazzi had emptied three cups before the star couple entered the street. They walked side by side on the pavement in front of the bookstore chatting and giggling. Elaine wore a sage-green sock dress, which emphasized her recently wildly trimmed figure. A curly cloud of hair framed her face. Red-rimmed sunglasses and rainbow-coloured sneakers embroidered Texaa's dark attire. When the love-doves were only a stone's throw away from their destination the secret shooter zoomed his camera on them. He would capture his photos at the point of the bookshop. That way they would be as iconic as they ever could be. He was just picking up the speed when a light-coloured van pulled up to a free parking spot in front of him blocking the view worth a fortune. When he sprung up, he heard a camera clicking on the driver's side and saw… George Bamby! He was capturing the couple out of the open window. The Finn tried to get there with all his might and means, elbowing the other customers, overturning and shaking bottles and crockery, to circle around the obstacle and get to the same fishing ground with his toughest competition. In looser waters he was faced with a nasty sight: the couple had fled too far away. The distance was so long that it was not worth his while to try to make another move. The van had turned on its flashers sliding into the traffic flow. The situation was over.

In a quarter of an hour the bitterly disappointed shooter got a message. "Hello, Papparazzi! You've done a fairly good job in here, but in our international match England scored again! Best wishes, George Bamby."

HIDDEN IN THE JUNGLE

The Swedish-born MaxAppSon, who was the brightest social media star in the world, got married to the Italian-born Giana in the enchantedly illuminated Temperate House in Kew Gardens. The bride was also a beloved youtuber. The wedding was intimate, the invitation for the epic moment was for the nearest ones only. The prebooked professional photographers took care of the shooting, all the paparazzi in town had been kept out from the whole shebang. Nevertheless, Papparazzi had an invitation in the tux pocket he had rented for the occasion. Acquiring the copy had taken many twists and turns. He had also disassembled his camera hiding the parts in his clothes. The wedding ring had been put on the bride's wedding finger in Nash Conservatory a while ago and at this point the guests were enjoying their festive dinner in the Temperate House. The crasher lurked outside the building trying to psych himself up to get past the hellhounds guarding the door. According to the programme information, the celebrants had a cocktail hour after the dinner before the next numbers, which were the cutting of the cake and the first dance. After taking a deep breath, he set out to climb up the stairs meeting the gatekeepers. The other man in black asked Papparazzi to hand in his invitation. It was really easy. The duo didn't even bother to go through the guestlist at this point. The follow-up question was trickier.

"Why are you coming this late? They are already clearing the tables."

He explained that the lingo had played tricks on the Nordic Viking. They had taken the scenic route on arrival in the traditional London taxi before finding the right place. Papparazzi gave his answer in the most widely spoken language, aka bad English mixing some Swedish words he had come up with at the last minute.

"Well, no problem then! Better late than ever. Remember to hold on to your cake."

The Norse promised to do as requested and drink more coffee than any other guest. Once he entered the atmospherically lit parlour, he saw a huge long table. It was surrounded by exotic greenery, an excellent hiding place for him to assemble his camera when the time was right. Tarzan dived inside his jungle after fifteen minutes of his arrival trying to be as invisible as he ever could. He had brought the most luminous lens with him, since using the flashlight was out of the question per se. A soundless camera was also an inevitability in a gig such as this. Steady hands and a good posture helped in making a valid imprint. He had mentally rehearsed his actions beforehand. He made good use of them, as he creeped to work under the bushy tree. Pappy took his time between shots. When he was ready, he hid his camera again. Staying as unnoticed as possible he returned to the bright lights of the hallway. One of the ladies spotted him. Papparazzi hastily made up a story of him having a green thumb and therefore not being able to resist the temptation of smelling the aroma of the soil even in a fancy party like this, while he was cleaning his suit and shoes out of the dirt.

"Where are they serving the Absolut Vodka?" he cracked when he was in fact taking a beeline out of the party venue.

After passing the doormen, he overheard them pondering why the guest arriving last was leaving the party first. In his car he chose the best pictures on the top of the stack and sent them into the *London Star*. In an hour everybody else could take part in the wedding bliss of the most famous youtuber couple. In Papparazzi's mind the most appealing pictures were the ones where the lovebirds were in front of the cake, engaged in the ceremonial dance and exchanging kisses. The picture where the bride in her Sleeping Beauty dress squeezed the groom's butt gently.

Later on, in the official and romantic wedding video, found with the keywords Max and Giana – The Wedding, Papparazzi's face was visible in the darkness of the jungle at the time of 4.20. Tarzan had spotted himself there once or twice. After his honeymoon, MaxAppSon published a video full of fire and brimstone naming it *The Finnish Devil Again!* The scarf guy couldn't be bothered to watch it. The little birds had chirped him that the youtuber had given in it a less flattering picture of Papparazzi, his professional skills and the Finns in general.

I MET A MONSTER

Murray Freeman, the sports reporter of *The Sensation* magazine had asked Papparazzi to be his photographer on a gig starring multiple Mr Olympia champion Billy Dunn. The case in question was a tour promoting bodybuilding as a sport. This time they were making a show of just posing and bulging their muscles instead of competing. Murray requested the shooter to concentrate on the American Mr Olympia throughout the whole PR show. He was not the least bit interested in the other beefcakes. He kept on warning nonchalantly of some threatening elements attached to the event. He had managed to make some critical comments of the sport prior to the event. There were some misgivings whether you could consider it a sport at all. He had cast his spotlight on Mr Olympia himself, wondering if his muscles had swollen to their current dimensions with just eating oatmeal porridge. He had received some bitter feedback from the enthusiasts of the industry including the black champion himself. The muscular mountain's message to the journalist was that the only two things he could hold between his fingers were his pen and his little doodle.

"Should we be cautious of Mr Olympia on that basis? Is he a health threat?" Papparazzi enquired.

"Argh! The titan is just letting off steam. I just wanted you to know what's going on between the two of us."

"Dare I ask what kind of tone you are taking on him this time?"

"Constructively critical as before."

Papparazzi began his contractual work when the event climaxed as the multiple Mr Olympia walked onto the stage in front of the cheering audience. The posing top-to-toe-oiled Billy looked like a statue with a frozen smile on his face. Every muscle was well exposed. Shiny thongs barely covered the strategic areas and his veins bulged visibly. The roar around the superman was deafening Papparazzi's ears.

Abruptly the hero stiffened resembling a totem.

"Is the pencil dick who criticised me present?"

The crowd was confused, Murray lifted his hand hesitantly capturing everyone's gaze.

"You will never ever be writing another line about me!" the bodybuilder boasted as he was dashing, holding his fists up towards the reporter who took a high-speed escape from the scene.

Papparazzi rose to the occasion and shot the chase as well as he could in the crowd. Mr Olympia was bellowing at the top of his lungs when elbowing his way through it.

"Come on, daffodil, let's take a match, man against man! You are the kind of fragile lyricist I'll eat for my evening snack!"

Murray vanished out of sight but it didn't calm Billy down a bit:

"That Snufkin thinks this isn't sport at all... Reputedly I am a doped monster. Those kind of false presenters piss me off!"

Papparazzi had advanced himself into a good position and was getting close-ups from the hog. His mouth was foaming and his eyeballs seemed to pop out of their sockets at any minute.

It went without saying *The Sensation* didn't sweep the threats against their employer under the carpet, they started a media blizzard over it instead. It was condemned once and for all. The freedom of speech was too much appreciated to be sacrificed on the behalf of one upset hormonal monster. Let him be ashamed and regretful of his words if he ever had the guts to do that! The whole Kingdom began pondering whether bodybuilding should be even called a sport. Mr Olympia gave his own feisty statement on the other side of the pond in New York.

"Bodybuilding is a sport! Everyone saying otherwise should be burnt in the eternal flames of hell!"

His gaze was really stern as he pointed it out to the TV camera:

"FYI, British scribbler in your flower hat, God forgives, I do not! If you ever cross my path, whether it is a street or a forest road, I will beat the crap out of you!"

Papparazzi saw the clip and couldn't resist sending him in its aftermath a song called 'I Met a Monster' sung by a Finnish singing janitor Sepi Kumpulainen, equipped with an appropriate translation. In its lyrics it was stated that the monster was precisely met on the forest road. The recipient sent an emoji with a grinning sun in return.

THE GOLDEN BOY'S HAT TRICK

An atmosphere of a great sport festival was taking on at the Jubilee Sports Ground. Liverpool, the champions of the Premier League, had invited the representatives of the media to the football field in order to reveal a piece of mega-class news. Papparazzi had also gotten commissions from multiple publications. Since it was taking place on Saturday, and as it happened his daughter Julia was visiting London for the weekend, the grandpa had taken the grandkids Nella and Eeli along with him. The parents were on a tour around the city with Edna during the event. The players were gathering on the field divided into the white and the red team. There was also a Teletubby with his black long hair wearing a red shirt with a legendary number Ten flashing on his back. The Grandpa Gang grasped immediately that the big secret the team had so carefully guarded was this fire-extinguisher-sized player. Cameras out now!

The exhibition match began in front of thousands of spectators. The ball stayed like it was glued to the feet of the long-haired speeder. He mocked the other players passing them like they were slalom poles. Once in a while he slipped cleverly through between their legs. The only way they seemed to get access to the ball was to play foul. The crowd started to buzz and cheer the wonder boy who was fast, agile and strong, it grew louder and louder by the minute. Once they had played for a quarter of an hour and the little Messi had made a hat trick, the referee blew at his whistle. The show was over.

The prodigy emerged on the edge of the field with the representatives of the team and, judging by their body language, the boy's father. Also, other interested parties were drawn to reporters and photographers in order to find out what the commotion was all about. The newsletter Papparazzi had grabbed told that Liverpool FC Academy had signed a deal with the six-year-old Iranian football player Kaveh Darabi. The chairman of the club Tim Kennedy praised Kaveh generously.

"As we all just saw, Kaveh was unstoppable even to the players of our champion team. At this point he has first-rate skills but by his age and size he'll have to wait for his debut in the men's league."

The aim was that he would become "at that memorable moment" the youngest player ever in the Premier League. The milestone would be reached in around ten years.

Kaveh's father Meghad told them his son's special talent appeared when he was only three months old.

"He possessed so much firmness and crispness that me and my wife decided to enrol him into an acrobatics and gymnastic school. Since then, he has taken on multiple forms of exercise. One year ago, he chose football as his priority."

The wonder boy's favourite players were Lionel Messi and Cristiano Ronaldo.

"As an adult he wants to be a more skilled player than them," Meghan emphasized.

The rest of the family had moved to Liverpool with the little Messi. The other members of the family had focused their lives and energy solely into ensuring their son had all the chances to become an outstanding professional. He was training two or three times a day. The living room had been transformed into a practice ground. The father was mostly happy that the super talent had a good-natured and bright disposition. The prodigy's face was glowing with joy when he took out his shirt and revealed his chilly sixpack. The Grandpa Gang had the front row seats for taking pictures of it.

Tim read the last row of the newsletter where Iran's captain of the football team thanked God for his blessed gift to his country in the form of Kaveh.

"Some day he'll be making the winning score in to the rival's net in the World Cup finals without needing Maradona's divine hand to help him out."

Tim had yet another announcement to give.

"As it was said in the newsletter, the children are also welcomed. Why? Because FC Liverpool is offering a slime party to the little ones in the family with appropriate delicacies. Kaveh will be a glowing star in the festivities as well. It's slime time, kiddies!" he cheered and gestured them to find their places among the dozens of tables brought near the field during the show game.

Eeli and Nella dashed to have fun with the rest of the crowd. The grandpa was trying to heel them with all of his capability. The tables were loaded with slime in Liverpool colours. Guidance was also available if needed. It didn't take long for the Finnish children to transform into red and white slimeballs dancing to the disco music and throwing balls at each other. Papparazzi took some hits from the elastic goo himself.

In the heat of the carousing the Grandpa Gang was able to go and take some pictures of Liverpool's newest enlisted player. They were top quality due to him being as thrilled with the festivities as the bright eyes. The grandpa found it hard to believe that the Iranian shared the same year of birth as Nella. The handler seemed to be more mature than his age.

"How does it feel to be a big star already?" she pried.

Once the grandpa and Meghad had interpreted he gave his answer.

"Really good! You and your brother can also join my fan group on social media!"

Nella promised to think about it.

"How many followers do you have?"

"Millions! And there's more joining in all the time. Only space is the limit!"

"Do you have dreams other than being a sports hero?"

"Getting a girlfriend!"

Meghad added that there would be no time for a girlfriend even when the next decade was due. The attention would be focused on the wrong things.

"Just keep your eye to the ball, my boy!"

Their chat session was interrupted maybe far too harshly by the other partygoers. After all, Eeli had only got to roll his eyes. The disappointment vanished quickly once the kids hit the pleasures of the table: cupcakes, popcorn, candies, chocolate cakes, waffles, sodas et cetera. As they were leaving, they received a slime jar with a Liverpool logo on it. Pappy made sure that they also got an autograph from Kaveh as a memento of the occasion. If ever the slime would be used in Finland, the slip with the autograph should be kept intact somewhere safe. In years to come it might be worth a fortune.

ROOM ONE-O-FIVE, ARRIVE THERE PLEASE

Papparazzi was lurking in the L-shaped recess with a doorless closet and some cleaning gear stashed in the back of room one hundred and five of the Royal Guest House. He was lured there by a famous TV personality/news presenter Regina Tilton after getting a sleazy message from the opposition leader Leith Charnley. The politician had enquired whether Regina was interested in playing a submissive role in an S&M session. At first the recipient had wanted to catch the two-timing politician in the act, but then she decided to entrap the guy. In her response message she announced being warmed up to the suggestion immediately and having booked a love nest in Shepherd's Bush for the two of them for twenty-four hours. In room one-o-five they could fulfil their wildest fantasies together. Whatever happens in the hotel would stay there. Or rather here since both of them were already chattering and tinkering on the spot.

The shooter listened attentively to the exchange between the master and the submissive. He was able to catch only a word or two from the murmur. The politician was no spring chicken in the act due to his numerous naughty encounters in between his busy life and housewife. The threshold of suggesting this kind of action to his wife Prunella was far too high, forcing him to seek his playmates elsewhere. He had followed Regina with that in mind for a while now. On the basis of magazine articles and interviews on TV he had deduced her feminism being just an act.

In fact, all the TV star wanted was a decent spanking on her bum from the master. The victim chuckled and demanded the master open his briefcase. This was the prearranged signal between Papparazzi and Regina. On the click he rushed to the doorway leading to the actual room on the partition wall raising the camera in front of his face. He was shooting pictures at a fiery pace. In the first frame, Leigh in his shirtsleeves was holding a chain, a whip and handcuffs in his hand mouth open with astonishment, Regina lying on the bed in a seductive nightie all pressed and powered. Her gaze was focused on the full-size mirror covering the wardrobe door on the opposite wall. In the open briefcase there were other sinful playthings and erotic clothing in working order. In five seconds, after dozens of pictures, the ruler fired up to the shooter using the f-word in a way that would have turned even the Top Chef Gordon Ramsay into a green fried tomato. In the last frame the Member of Parliament standing behind the bed tried to go after Papparazzi and Regina who had grabbed her overcoat from the night stand.

In no time the runaways were on the Shepherd's Bush Road taking a turn on the right heading towards The Richmond Pub. While they were a long way off, they dared to stop and look back. The opposition leader was nowhere to be seen on the pavement. He had either taken a different direction or was still licking his wounds in the one-o-five. Regina had left her purse, make-up and outer garments so she decided to get the reception to sort things out. After turning to the staff, she had nothing to worry about. She intended to make some white lies about her unusual costume and events at the hotel room in order to come clean. After regaining her belongings, her next goal was to head straight home. Papparazzi headed to his car listening on the returning trip to Kikka's hit song 'Room One-O-Five': "When you first winked at me, So was the dance a follow-on to the play, I was showing green to you, And deep fervour already took place... I have a hideaway for you, There you can join me. Room one-o-five Arrive there please Paapaadiidappappa..."

In Pimlico the Finn put the big gear on. Since he was now working on his own behalf the highest bidder would get the pictures. The buyer could have the exclusive rights to them. Regina didn't want any monetary compensation for the business as her only goal was to uncover the dirty games of the two-faced politician to the public and above all to Prunella. When the bait was thrown in the media field the offers started pouring in. *London Star* wanted to get the photos but they ran out of money on the first round. *Inland News* began the game with a bid of fifty thousand. It made the seller's blood move and made his breathing heavier, but he decided to sit on his hands just in order to avoid clicking his acceptance of them. In an hour *The Sensation* added oil to the fire by offering sixty-five thousand. The curly still played the waiting game. At nine p.m. an American media consortium *Viva Global*, who also had its own publication channels in the UK, cleared the table offering a balanced bid. One hundred thousand dollars were on the table only for five more minutes, making the other options scarce. Game over!

Soon after receiving the photos *Viva Global* spread them efficiently around the world although the highest waves of the media storm were foaming in Britain. Regina was giving the first announcements of her traumatic experience. She was outraged at the double life led by a politician ranting about Christian family values. The pure suggestion of the S&M had made her fall on her bum.

After the incident and having his tendencies leaked to the public, Leith took sick leave. He didn't give any comments to the shooters and reporters surrounding him. The silent treatment couldn't stop the inquisitive journalists finding out his tendency to approach several women with similar conditions for a number of years. The hide-and-seek game with the media and the MeToo movement ended, when Mr Paparazzi Darren Lyons caught the opposition leader unforgettably. He was making a trip to the nearby convenience store hiding inside his official car's trunk and got busted. The pictures were embarrassing even for the most faithful advocates of the politician. The top notch should always be seen standing upright holding his head up and not as a spineless animal avoiding his responsibilities. Leith promised to step out of the party leadership and take on his backbench membership in Parliament as of now. In his silence-breaking statement he apologised for all the distress he had caused to Regina and all the women he had oppressed in his obscene games. "I made heavy mistakes. I admit. I regret. The media and feminists have taken me on my knees totally. The list of my sins is a mile long. I plead forgiveness from all I have hurt. I have no idea of the number. Even one is too many!"

TOP MODELS RIP OFF

The mother of punk fashion/fashion designer Tiffany Haselwood, the lifestyle boutique Kitson from Los Angeles and Edna brainstormed the March of Openwork T-shirts photo expo to the Snow White Gallery. Top models from the UK and USA featured punk-spirited torn T-shirts with slogans printed on them. Many of them also had shredded jeans on. The most thrilling part of the whole thing was the fact that the models had been able to choose their own slogans freely. Once this was announced in the modelling world, the supply exceeded demand multiple times over on both sides of the pond. The models were fascinated by the chance of performing in a visual artwork. It also gave Papparazzi the possibility to take his time shooting them. All in all, the whole shebang had taken about six months to finish. The most memorable ones were the ones taking place in Los Angeles and New York since they were a nice change from London. The only absolute requirement was that the whole slogan should appear completely in the photos. There were thirty pictures on display in Piccadilly.

The expo opening made big headlines. Due to the limitations of the space the list of invites was handpicked. The representatives of UK and US top medias, the models and the London socialites overflowed the place. Mandi was also a part of the buzz – she was capturing photos of the opening festivities and the main stars to Edna and Papparazzi. Most of them would end up in their home albums and some of them would make good promotional material. The interviews and the presentations were taking so much of the power couple's time that Pappy hadn't bothered to take his camera to the Piccadilly Arcade. The women's magazine *Mellow* had booked him to talk about the pictures for the first half an hour. Reporter Nydia Fling and photographer Willa Matkin captured him with them immediately after the opening speeches and toasts. The tour began with a picture taken in Manhattan where in the midst of the crowd stood out Clark Eames, best known from *The Sex and The City*, wearing a red T-shirt. He had played the role of an underwear model called Derek. On top of his naked belly button was showing off a text: "My dick is my only weapon!" At once Nydia connected the statement with the liberal arms carrying policy making a jogging black man find himself in a life-threatening situation. As if they were trying to escape the police. Papparazzi admitted her deduction to be the right one.

"Mass shootings are taking place daily in the US. Most of the occurrences don't even make it to the headlines. Something has to be done eventually. We need more action and less rhetoric," the scarf man interpreted his subject's message.

"I'm wondering whether he ever thought using the word dick through in this context?"

"As a true player he understands the importance of making a point, if you want it to shock and awe the largest possible number of recipients."

"Anyway, it's making an aggressive and offensive feeling. For some women it is too big a word to be swallowed."

"I'll answer to that like the Savonians say in my country: maybe or maybe not."

His comment excited laughter in both women. Willa asked Papparazzi to pose beside the artwork. Say cheese in order to make your facial expression more amiable and shots from different angles. It was obvious from the beginning that she was a true professional in her own right.

"What kind of a man is Clark?" the reporter asked.

"We didn't have much to do with each other outside the shooting but we went for a cup of coffee once. I got an impression that he is a charming and rather pleasant guy. His involvement in the T-shirt business gives me more assurance that his text choice was carefully considered."

"What a coincidence!"

"Exactly! That's why he is displayed here in such magnitude. The other thing is that he is flying the flag for humanity and love!"

"Great guy!"

At Oxford Circus underground post, Nina Colt charmed with her hands risen to the sky. There were multiple holes in her white T-shirt, the most eye-catching of them was teasingly revealing the areola of her left breast. The slogan of the supermodel was "Wake up!" It was printed in black.

"How should we understand this pair of words?" Willa pondered as she was shooting with her gear.

"It is rather ambiguous but when I had a conversation with the supermodel herself, she revealed wanting to awaken people to use their own brains. There are too many people doing just the opposite."

"That is actually a very thought-provoking comment spiced with eroticism," Nydia uttered.

"I must admit things got heated when I was shooting her. My camera loved her. Although her speech was so blurred that I suspected she was high on something."

"She could very well have smoked out. Drugs have been a

problem to her for a while now. Nina has been in rehab several times over but the drug scandals keep following on her heels nevertheless."

Willa memorised Nina being attached to the royalty of British rock Liam Gallagher with whom she had made out in the past.

"There is a paparazzo image drawn on my retinas of him throwing a beer glass towards the queen of catwalks. Yuck!"

The trio moved on to the next creations. On the stairs in front of the Royal Albert Hall posed the black stunner Miranda Aduddell. The threesome studied the creation with great care. A glowing golden text on a black shirt proclaimed the Gospel of sex: "Sex, Drugs, Hunks and Rock'n'roll!" The message was so clear that you had to be braindead not to notice it.

"She must be a man-eater judging by the looks the dudes threw at her when we were shooting. Other than that, her foul mouth caused more commotion in the crowd around her. She has litigated with paparazzi all the time and I was not spared either from her sharp tongue. She described me as being a boil in need of bursting with violence if needed. My presence on the spot she tolerated only because Tiffany is one of her best friends."

It was obvious the little love between them had affected the end result.

"Her pose in this picture looks a bit off. As if she was falling down and needed a supporting banister to keep her steady, but it's lacking from this picture," Nydia noted.

"The artistic impression is very good because of that. Me liking!" Willa played along.

The camera shutter was flashing again. When the photographer was finished at that point, they went up the stairs where the expo continued. Once they got through the crowd, they stopped in front of the artwork called *The Fantastic Man*. In the picture the model Benjamin Duhaime carried his ragged clothes with pride with a cigarette tucked behind his ear and the dial of Big Ben behind him.

"He really is a fantastic man. The sight still gives me the creeps," the reporter gloated.

Afterwards Benjamin had revealed that Big Ben meant more to him than the Finn could ever imagine. To him it symbolised England and London, the sign of hope. That's why he had chosen to be photographed in close proximity to it.

"The hunk has beautiful thoughts," Willa proclaimed as she was using her camera.

That wasn't the last of the tourist attractions of London. Papparazzi was very keen to present also a photo he had taken from Buckingham Palace where the red-coated guard stood upright and pokerfaced – at the same time as a beauty in her torn T-shirt tried to make his head spin with her flirtation. The message was: "Fashion makes the world better."

"My countrywoman Iina Loponen has already made it here, but you two haven't met her yet."

"No, we haven't – except now we have of course. Cool dreadlocks!"

Click, click!

On the famous Sunset Boulevard in Los Angeles, Ann Walker, the model and actress who had once been ranked to be one of most beautiful women in the world, revealed her message: "You can be you and I can be me."

Nydia's pen froze. It took her a while before she was able to cough up:

"The top star has a perfect look on her face. And something important to say. How would you simplify it in other words,

Papparazzi?"

"Never push your jaw down, forget your dreams or blend into the grey mass. Keep your head proudly upright."

"You just blew my mind!"

"Thank you! Ann was one of the best subjects in this alluring set. The camera loved her natural exposure so much it was filled up within ten minutes of the exposure."

"My equipment is also crammed! The photo part of the expo is excellent," Willa stated.

Nydia asked her last question in Columbo's style.

"What is the most memorable thing about Annie to you personally?"

"Unfortunately, she couldn't make an appearance here today – that being the case you could have asked her. So I answer you that it was her height. Especially when wearing those high heels, she was a head taller than anyone else walking down the Sunset Boulevard."

The working couple thanked Papparazzi for the rewarding presentation before rushing to mingle in with the rest of the crowd. The duo intended to access the works not included in the tour. Edna was standing beside the blond while giving statements to the American TV station. She overheard her pressuring the fact that the organizers had been given the honour of picking the best of the best from a really representative sampling, the peak of the iceberg, to the expo. The ensemble would then travel to Los Angeles where Kitson would squeeze every last dollar out of it. At this point, most of the creations were being sold but the buyers had agreed to get them just after the show in Hollywood. By now it was the time to wipe off all the presumptions of models – lacking heart and brains – both of them were found in them so plentifully that there were no words left to describe them. She unfolded her arms to point out the fact.

Mandi tapped the expo photographer's shoulder. As the lovebirds were conveniently standing side by side, she had captured a bunch of pictures of them in the middle of the buzz. She craved more now together with Papparazzi, since it was apparent that Edna couldn't be able to draw herself out of the media representatives any time soon. It meant another tour around the expo – but not before a refill. The tables were laid up with all kinds of sweet and savoury snacks which Papparazzi and Mandi enjoyed with pleasure. They also had a few gin and tonics. The free flow of alcohol went on very well making some guests quite pasted. Pappy expressed regrets because this expo was not marching on to Gallery Papparazzi in Helsinki.

"Of course I made an effort to get it there as well due to my own agenda, but for several reasons it wasn't meant to happen. The collectors wanted to get access to their purchases as soon as possible."

"The photos will be selling like hot buns in the future as well."

The scarf guy changed the subject; he was anxious to know how the other businesses were going. Especially shooting the commoners as being celebrities, since it had gotten a flying start before his departure to London.

"Me and Machine tried to keep the wheels running with it for a while, but it just didn't work. We would have needed some extra hands but we didn't have the means to do it. Nobody wanted the sudden alerts and odd hours of work."

"There was this keen and technically competent lad in Oulu… What was his name?"

"Lassi Karvonen. Bringing him to Helsinki would have required a lot of arrangements on both sides so we decided to pass."

"Maybe we'll be able to revitalise that part of our business someday."

"If you mean your romance with the most beautiful English Rose, let me be straight: it happens only in your dreams!"

Papparazzi got lost in his thoughts. Returning home felt more farfetched than ever. A top-notch job and a booming relationship glued him tighter and tighter to London. This was the time to ask the question that had been nagging at him for a while now.

"Why did you originally warn me off Edna? I mean her being a nymphomaniac..."

She burst into the heartiest laughter. When she was able to stop her giggling, she revealed jokingly:

"We plotted it together, or rather Edna did, once she had set her eyes on you when you stepped into this gallery for the first time. As she learned more of you, she knew that if she ever would attract your attention, she had to take more drastic measures. In her attention-and-love-seeking she turned to me – and the rest is history. Judging by everything, she has managed to lasso you very near to her!"

The blond couldn't help but laugh about it. Women! But a hefty man couldn't have a life without them.

"How is the Machine doing nowadays?"

"We haven't been really in close touch recently. He is involved in some sort of recycling business. By the way, his dilapidated Suzuki car has now kicked the bucket."

"May she rest in peace! We haven't been in contact with each other either. I'll be fixing the situation right away."

"Do it! As I have gathered, he is lonely. He hasn't even managed to get himself a new car yet."

"About that... How is your love life these days?"

"No news from that front yet!" Mandi blurted hiding her blushing cheeks behind her camera.

That side of the gallerist's life was now dealt with. He turned the subject of the conversation to the Gallery Papparazzi since it was doing so well. Stockholm's most established female paparazzo Bea Stolpe had opened her expo a week ago called Greetings from the Bush! and it brought a lot of visitors in. There were some people coming in the Runeberginkatu all the way from Sweden, which was especially gratifying. Some purchases had also been made. All this was a symphony to Papparazzi's ears.

Tiffany sailed through the crowd to join them in her flashy shirt with a print: "Punk Is Always In Fashion!"

Papparazzi felt a prick in his guts. He, Mandi and Edna, who had joined their company, had dressed up for the occasion in casually festive attires. Shirts with holes in them would have been more appropriate costumes in this event. As if the creator of the punk fashion had anticipated the expo photographer's thoughts she pronounced:

"If you had a shirt in line with the theme too, what would you have written on it, Pappy?"

It had to be considered for a moment.

"Maybe something like 'Sixpack Coming Soon'!"

"That's wonderful. How about you, Edna?"

Another reflection period was on again. It hadn't occurred to her to exert herself on her own slogan beforehand and now she was summoned. The severity factor was sufficient. She took Papparazzi's hand and whispered hoarsely:

"'Hand in Hand We Hit The Same Chords'!"

Tiffany was overjoyed.

"What words would you like to wear, Mandi?"

"My message would be that there is art in everything. 'Where goes the line between art and life? They are all the same'!"

"Wow! That was deep!"

Tiffany had scrutinised all the exhibition pictures with a magnifying glass. She was bursting with enthusiasm when describing the expo with her words. As her favourite she mentioned a photo taken in the British Museum where the glamour model Crystal Dice touched the case covering the Rosetta Stone wearing a T-shirt with a print: "The Stone Opens Its Innermost."

"Crystal was the only person refusing to wear a ripped shirt. A sleeveless top was her only concession," Papparazzi made his own little anecdote behind the scenes.

"Crystal can be stubborn. An exception that proves the rule. The picture touches perfection, it has the message!"

The picture taker agreed its being a direct hit. Why had he left it out of the selected images he had offered to the reporter and photographer of the Mellow? At this point he couldn't comprehend it at all. He must have dozed off. The fashion guru went on:

"This expo is so punk! Safety pins and pins should be presented more in the pictures – like back in the days when we rocked this island and the world. We as punks wanted and still want to stir with a giant spoon the social circles and numbed braincells. Nothing proceeds in still waters."

Papparazzi admitted being a friend of the trend himself. Punk had been his number one thing as a young and not-so-angry man.

"If all the punk records would be bunched up and only one

was left to exist, it would be the Sex Pistols' *Never Mind The Bollocks*."

"Cheers, Paps! The foul-mouthed and snotty air-heads of London got it right somehow after all!"

Affirmative nods and humming surrounded them like the halo of the saint. This sweet serenity was disturbed by Miranda who had had her fair share of booze during the night. A tight dress was barely covering her private parts. Even her expression was so tight that it was obvious she was hatching anger and pitch-black venom inside – looking for an outlet. The volcano activated fast beyond anyone's expectations.

"Thanks for nothing, asshole Papparazzi, for the way you present me in that photo you have chosen to display! I look like a tottering junkie and the most used floozie of the city. I'll kick your arse!"

A Guess design handbag swished against the scarf guy's face. When Miranda's hand raised for the second blow – miss! Next one… Tiffany, Mandi, Edna and many others dashed to create a covering wall around the punk pap. The attacker's eyes rushed with fire and murder and all the soothing words fell on deaf ears. Even those Tiffany made concerning the beaten-up photo having a strong sexual charge in it. The photographers from the TV companies and newspapers were witnessing the assault in a jiffy. On their tails a bunch of mobile phones were raised to capture it. Pappy was punk'd again!

THE TEN BELLS MYSTERY

On Friday night The Ten Bells pub was packed. Apart from the entertainment it also provided a shelter from the rainfall out on the Commercial Road in Spitalfields. Papparazzi had arrived on the spot at the request made by The London Dungeon and Graham. The tourist attraction was organizing a new show about Jack the Ripper, and the Ten Bells was going to be the main forum of it. Since the main attraction was still under finishing work, the photographer had been summoned to enter the actual pub. The player acting the serial killer would also be there in plain clothes at first and later on playing the part. The scarf guy was supposed to pick the right one from the crowd. The commissioner of the job wanted to mess with him. The dungeon also wanted to test the credibility of the character. In order to ease the job, he had been told that the performer was born to the part of the perpetrator of the bloody tasks. Papparazzi had risen to the challenge due to him having read the book by Russell Edwards and Jari Louhelainen on the subject. According to the book, the brutal killer was revealed as being a Polish Jew called Aaron Kosminski. The evidence of his culpability was strong. So Papparazzi had scrutinised Kosminski's facial features from the multiple drawings he had found from the internet. He was a dark man with moustache, sideburns and withdrawn hairline. He also had a protruding big nose, strong jaw, eyes buried into the sockets and hollow cheeks. With these characteristics he would recognise the knife wielder immediately, when he saw him. Papparazzi had taken a perfect spot near the entrance and the bar. None of the people entering or leaving would miss his hawk eye. He seized the moment with a frosty in front of him.

The old-fashioned pub ambiance labelled The Ten Bells due to its existence in the same spot for centuries. Jack the Ripper had with a high probability visited the pub, the strongest connections with it were two of his victims Annie Chapman and Mary Jane Kelly. All the so-called certain victims had been Mary Ann Nichols, Elizabeth Stride and Catherine Eddowes. The bloody murders took place in 1888 and the press had given them a lot of attention at the time. The sensational journalism had taken its baby steps back then. Without the fatal strikes all of the women would have vanished into the endless night of oblivion, now their memory would live on. The murders in Whitechapel had also touched Jack London, the American author, who had later on entered the same hoods dressed as a raggedy man. *The People of the Abyss: A Narration of the East End of London* had been published in 1903. In the eyes of the poor the society had seemed to be a gigantic flattening machine pressing them constantly and inevitably lower towards the rock bottom. Such a heavy quantity of despair made Papparazzi's blood run cold. Extreme poverty was a more hideous crime than any that Jack the Ripper had ever committed, no-one should ever be victimised with it. In a perfect world there were no poor people, but since the world was far from perfect, the poverty was still an issue.

He noticed a guy with a spitting image of the Ripper in the back of the room. Where did he come from? Maybe from the cocktail bar upstairs? It was time to solve the puzzle! He had no choice but to take the camera bag on his shoulder and step forward. Papparazzi greeted the easy-going lad cheerfully:

"Jack the Ripper, I presume?"

The guy was puzzled wanting to know what the hell he was talking about. Papparazzi repeated the question failing to get the correct answer. He assumed his abilities as Sherlock were being tested so he decided to add pressure to his enquiries.

"It's you who is trying to fool me. You are the uncrowned King of the underworld – just admit it!"

Once Papparazzi managed to get his camera out, the suspicious creep got scared. He gestured the bartender to help him. A heated discussion went on a bit before everyone realised it was the shooter who had messed up everything. The lad's name was also Jack but that was the only connection to the horror figure. Nevertheless, his honour had been bloodily insulted. The Finn refunded the inconvenience by buying him a cold beer; and another one since the lad continued to have suspicious eyes.

The time ticked on and Jack did not stand out in a crowd. Had he made a fatal mistake in thinking that Aaron Kosminski was the villain in the new display? He started to fiddle with his phone fiercely. George Chapman, David Cohen, Thomas Cutbush, Montague Druitt, Jacob Levy, Walter Sickert... All of a sudden, surprisingly, several guys in the crowd seemed to tick all the boxes of the criminal from hell he was looking for. Jacob Levy passed by, a moustached man resembling Francis Tumblety was on his way down... The detective was anything but on the heels of the crook, he was in dire straits! A temper tantrum was on its way. As everything was looking bleak, a dark-haired woman popped out to him. She had a white-powdered face, crimson lips and eyebrows resembling raven wings.

"Are you Papparazzi, the one who has been between a rock and a hard place more than once?"

The shooter nodded.

"I just couldn't wait any longer for you to spot me so I took the initiative into my own hands. I am… Jackie the Ripper! Hello stranger!"

The knight of the round table almost fell off his chair by surprise. What the hell? Was somebody trying to pull his leg? The bartender, who had earlier spoken to him tightly, waved his hand behind the counter.

"I almost revealed the secret of The Ten Bells me and Jackie the Ripper fostered, when you worked your way to the first suspect. Fortunately, I could keep a straight face! Now the mystery is solved. Here's to that, the drinks are on the house. What can I get you?"

Jackie the Ripper ordered a vodka shot and Papparazzi changed his beer to whisky. The photographer wanted to hear the whole story from the maiden sitting next to him.

"While investigating the doings of Jack the Ripper, the police discovered that the murderer might be female. That line of inquiries was never opened. Only recently a former attorney John Morris did it, ending up with the conclusion that the perpetrator behind the murders was Lizzie Williams. She murdered the women because she couldn't have children of her own."

"That's interesting! Please do go on!"

"Lizzie was the wife of the Court Physician John Williams. He has also been suspected of being Jack the Ripper ever since the knife found in his estate was fit for a murder weapon. Maybe Lizzie used the knife instead of John? According to detectives there were several feminine characteristics in the killings. For example, the removing of the uterus pointed at that direction. And none of them was raped. Mary Jane Kelly was intentionally the last victim. Kelly and Williams had an affair and the wife took her revenge by killing the mistress."

The shooter whistled and then revealed to the new Jackie the

Ripper the version he believed to be true i.e. the perpetrator was Aaron Kosminski.

"The DNA Scientist and Molecular Biologist Jari Louhelainen, who by the way is my compatriot, found Kosminski's DNA from the scarf belonging to Jack the Ripper's fourth victim Catherine Eddowes. There was semen, blood and remains of a kidney. Eddowes was missing a kidney when she was found torn to shreds. I take this as being strong evidence of Kosminski's guilt. The killings of the women stopped, when he was committed to the mental institution."

"What were his motives?"

"Misogynism and murderous tendencies. He lived near the crime scenes and he had been known to threaten at least two women with a knife."

Incisive gazes pointed to the bottoms of the empty glasses. There were no words describing human cruelty. The brunette pulled their thoughts out of the deep valley back to the rogue lights of the pub by announcing that she was going into The Lounge upstairs in order to get into Jackie the Ripper's armour.

"We are here to take pictures and not ponder on grim thoughts!" she announced on her way up.

When she returned there was a convulsion in the pub. A top hat, a shoulder cape with a large collar, sleeves down to the knuckles, a red silk blouse, an ankle-length skirt and Pompadour styled shoes did their job. A blood-stained butcher knife clenched into Jackie the Ripper's hands completed the picture. Papparazzi made the shutter of his camera click fiercely. He fired the final pictures of the dangerous woman through the objective outside, since the rain had ceased during the evening. Jackie the Ripper lit her cigarette, and they started pondering, who would draw the longest straw in the case of the most notorious serial killer. When

Jackie the Ripper finished smoking, they agreed to surrender in front of the case and departed to their separate ways. Jack the Ripper – not forgetting the female suspects – played such a big part of the gigantic entertainment industry that finding out the true identity of the murderer would not benefit anyone. Ever.

A FUNNY THING HAPPENED ON THE RED CARPET

The atmosphere in front of luxury store Gucci at the Westfield shopping mall intensified when three-year-old Mirella Ross started her walk on the red carpet. Mirella was famous for wearing only expensive designer clothing when she appeared to the public. In this case, she was going to wear them on the catwalk starring in the show. The shopping mall had arranged for her a private facility where she was able to change her clothes with the help of her mother Lizzie. Papparazzi was invited on the scene in order to capture the memorable moment. Since Julia had brought her family to London again, the grandpa had decided to give Nella and Eeli a proper do or die moment. The grandpa had not even taken his own shooting gear; he was just sitting back and watching them hovering around the model with their cameras. The fashion model of Gucci walked slowly giving the members of the public all the chances to capture as many elegant pictures of her as possible. As well as being a fashion icon, Mirella was a popular social media influencer. Lizzie was relentlessly producing more and more content about her daughter's life making her way to Hollywood stardom.

    As Mirella was posing with a Moschino bronzy jacket, the crowd made a rushing stiff breeze. In the middle of everything a tabby cat emerged on the carpet making it a real catwalk. The cat took his time in washing himself and then took off to padding in the direction of the little girl. His intention was obvious: he wanted to capture the public's undivided admiration for himself. So he began to shoo the model out of his way with his paw. She lost her step and fell on her knees in front of Nella and Eeli. They utilised the situation with efficiency making Papparazzi full of pride. The cash would be pouring in. As opposite to the professional stages where the models rushed to get up as quickly as possible in order to go on walking, Mirella acknowledged her stumble by staying on the carpet chuckling – holding the cat on her lap. Nobody knew where the cat had emerged. Nobody claimed its ownership. When the girl had taken her time patting and scratching him, he vanished into the crowd as quickly as he had appeared.

Although everybody seemed to feel exceptionally nice after the incident the show was brought to completion with honours. The tiny model was visibly relaxed pulling up her weight, her smile being her greatest asset.

IN THE VORTEX OF LAUGHTER

In the big world the citizens of the small Finland closed ranks. Currently in The Freemasons Arms pub stand-up comedian Ismo Leikola and Papparazzi did it with some snacks and beer. Ismo wanted Papparazzi to shoot photos of his gig later that evening at the Soho Comedy Club. The photographer had instantly agreed to do it, although he suspected that, in spite of having been named as the funniest person in the world, this gig would not get any attention in the London press at all. Ismo got that but was eager to get some of the best shots into his own collection. He could utilise them on his homepage. He also wanted to know what was required to make him stand out. In Papparazzi's opinion, nothing less than taking off his pants or setting himself on fire on the stage would do the trick. Nevertheless, he didn't encourage his compatriot to act on it. The comedian had an enigmatic expression on his face, when he suggested that Papparazzi and his sweetheart Edna should stay put until the end of the shebang just in case. The shooter promised to do it. He also showed a passport photo of his sweetie pie to the star.

"You'll be seeing her alive later this day."

"You mustn't slip away without coming to greet me after the show!"

In past years Ismo had mostly performed in the US. The comparison between American and Finnish lifestyles was one of his specialities. He also got laughs from the word ass. The competition of the limelight was hard but fair. He had defeated the English language. How different it was from their beloved mother tongue! Purely the fact how much the written and spoken English differed from each other made it very difficult to chew on to for the Finn. Papparazzi admitted he had noticed it himself as well. After a few months of using foreign language, he also was getting the hang of it.

"There are so many expats in London that they are making badly spoken English the most widely spoken language here," Ismo added with consolation.

"I agree, but you know what us Finns are like. We tend to avoid even the smallest mistake to the extent of keeping quiet rather than embarrassing ourselves."

"Been there, done that. I'm going to go into that in my show."

"I'll be all ears!"

The star promised that all aspects of human life would be present in his *Best of* show as they said goodbyes in front of the pub.

The audience in the comedy club was anxiously waiting to see the star of the night's appearance. The stage was tiny, there were a lot of seats for the audience and the service from the bar was fluent. Edna sat somewhere in the darkness. Papparazzi had sought a standing place near the edge of the stage – on the same side with the table and the water bottle on top of it. He had made an educated guess of the comedian preferring that side. Sped up by the host's glowing words, Ismo dashed on the mic grabbing it with trembling hands. He wore jeans and a plaited shirt on top of his tee. He made a beastly start by saying that dolphins had the brain capacity to build a similar civilisation as us humans. Why wouldn't they make the effort? Because they had fins instead of hands, unsuitable for construction work. The place roared with laughter.

"They cannot even hold a pen in their fins. So, goodbye the dream of becoming a writer. They must have been as fucked as a little squirrel seeing a frozen pinecone."

People jumped up and down with joy. And on it went with humans involved.

"As a man, I have noticed how unfairly my body expands. The fat is so unevenly deposited to my belly, arms, thighs, face... Even my toe can gain weight. But my damned weenie seems to decrease all the time, which isn't fair at any rate!"

Papparazzi took joyful pictures one after another. The first bawlers to the performer opened their mouths. The comedian turned up the heat by cutting into the strange hitches of the Finnish legislation. The official age limit for boozing is eighteen years, but still the young adult couldn't buy any stiff spirits from Alko.

"You can get stiff drinks in a public bar, but the legislator does not allow you to have it in the privacy of your own home. It makes you wonder if the bureaucrats have really thought this through, doesn't it?"

The second strange age limit in the law was that you can have sex at the age of sixteen but you have to be two years older in order to watch porn.

"So, if you film your own porn at the age of sixteen, it'll take two years before you are allowed to watch it. What's the point in that?"

Finding a sex partner is difficult to a single guy. If ever they found a compliant female, she would be allergic to rubber and leather.

"Then you'll have no choice but to get a woollen sock in between!"

The last strike was rewarded with roaring applauses. Ismo took a little sip of water chuckling absentmindedly. He turned to the crowd with a mischievous expression on his face.

"You English use secret letters in your language – you write them down but never pronounce them. Why don't you just stop writing all those unnecessary letters?"

As an example, Ismo used the word debt. In English it is written debt but pronounced det. At this point he let it loose altogether. Why on earth the countries owing a humongous amount of money took an effort of paying back to the creditors, since the first mentioned possessed the armed forces and the latter had only a few clerks and a cleaner in their offices? A state was capable of threatening their claimants with killing devices of all sizes, even with a nuclear weapon, when the banks were equipped with a stapler. Genghis Khan was also marched on the stage in order to pay back his student debts. When the office manager heard that there were thousands of armed-to-the-teeth soldiers supporting their leader, he decided to be inexplicably merciful letting the Great Khan leave with his wallet intact. But his credit rating would be black-listed in the database. The crowd was splitting their sides.

The comedian disappeared to get something behind the scenes. This time he didn't emerge with a guitar – having a habit of spicing up his act with humorous songs – but with a bucket.

"In the capitol of Northern Finland, Oulu, there was one theatrical performance beyond compare. That being the one when *The God's Theatre* threw crap on the audience. There were some leftovers from the festivities of the British Court. My friend from the cavalry was kind enough to hand me a bucketful of it. Now I'm taking the act of *God's Theatre* to you!"

He scooped some of the brown goo and threw it towards the

viewers. After a couple of throws the theatre crowd started to escape in full speed. Most of them were still in joyous mood, but none of those getting stains on their clothes were going to suffer in silence. The disgusting smell made them hold on to their noses as they were exiting. In the end, only Edna and a bespectacled elderly gentleman remained in their seats. Ismo got closer to the suits with his load.

"Didn't I raise any reaction in you at all?"

"No, you didn't! Just keep tossing that poop on me but I won't budge! That is to say I'll watch this show to the bitter end!"

Instead of making a gesture of targeting the old geezer he decided to let his shovel and bucket go. Papparazzi asked Edna to find out the name of the gentleman. It was obvious the photos of Ismo's *Best of* show's latest turn would get massive coverage in the media. The gentleman beating the crap out of the comedian was also under scrutiny. Fortunately, he gave his name to the lady as asked: the Ironsides was called Herbert Bellow from Luton. Edna, Ismo and Papparazzi chased to the backstage where the dressing rooms appointed to the comedians were. Once Ismo had stuffed his gear into his backpack they rushed out at breakneck pace – now in the direction of the exit. The managers and staff of the comedy club had no time to react in order to catch the vanishing perpetrator. At that point the escaping trio was already nearing Edna's condo. The lady speeded in the front, while the Finnish duo followed her closely. They had to make an effort to avoid the festive crowds on the street. The speed made their lungs burst. They had to endure, only one more bend to round…

A colourfully illuminated rickshaw with Union Jacks hanging on it jerked off near the home of the gallerist at Cambridge Circus. The green staircase door was opened and they quickly leaped up into safety. Nobody could find them there.

"We survived through London!" sweaty Ismo rejoiced.

"We could do the honours with some red wine, couldn't we?"

"Hell, yeah!" Papparazzi exclaimed.

While they were toasting, the comedian wanted to clarify what had really happened.

"Honestly, I didn't do a shit at the club! My aim was to throw the stuff just on the floor in front of the first row. I couldn't help them stepping on it as they shot on the move. Well, one or two turds might have landed on their tights, but that was all!"

Papparazzi and Edna were relieved hearing it. Putting it like that, the deed didn't seem that serious at all. They were eager to know the origins of the bucket with the brown contents.

"As I was leaving the Freemasons Arms, I got a recollection of the escapade *The God's Theatre* pulled off decades ago in Oulu. The actors had combined manure and art in a way of shaking every Finn to the core. I decided to pull the same striking stunt here today. It would be rakish enough to make me to gain visibility in local medias. All the other surprises I had come with were too blunt. I phoned accordingly to the nearest city-farm asking, if they could produce me some of the real stuff. No matter what animal had done its solid drop."

"And they proceeded?"

"Oh, yeah! The bucket with its contents were brought to me within an hour. I tipped the driver a hundred pounds. He was kind enough to let me keep the bucket."

"He was fair to you, mate!"

"He certainly was! Before my gig I went to the store and purchased a spade, since I didn't want to get my hands dirty."

As the poop prank was weighing on Ismo's conscience, he phoned Sebastian Carlson, who was the big guy of the comedy club in order to find out what he owed to the facilities. The phone conversation went smoothly and Ismo's facial expression went sunny as it proceeded. After finishing his gabbing Papparazzi and Edna were bursting with curiosity as to whether the phoners had reached consensus.

"The staff had taken down the contact information of the people with soiled clothes, mostly socks and stuff, in order for me to pay the laundry bills. Some of them may need to buy new shoes as well. None of the seats were contaminated and they're managing to clean the floor as we speak. Neither the club nor any of the disturbed viewers have any intention of reporting this to the police, so I will be shaken but not hurt by this divine performance!"

The entertainment artist avoided being banned from the club altogether as well.

"This was the first and the last performance with manure on the stage! That was the thing Sebastian made clear in plain language. I promised I would never ever pull a stunt like that on those premises again."

Papparazzi had assembled all the graphics software he needed on Edna's PC and went on to separate out the best poop-throwing images on display. It was obvious he had plenty of time to forward the photos to the blood-thirsty tabloids at first light. He had had exclusive rights on the shooting at Comedy Club. He had handpicked a set of twenty frames.

"I look like a raving madman in those!"

"These will sell like hot cakes. And don't forget to paint as colourful a picture to the extent that your nature will give in, when talking to the reporters tomorrow. The more pointed comments you make, the more extravagant headlines about the attack are. You can announce them having made a manifest of what stand-up could be or not be. Or just tell them, how a real artist lets the art speak for itself."

"Herbert will also give his own stamp on the affair too. He himself will be a real celebrity in his own right!" Edna enthused.

The trio agreed that Ismo's basic gig in the metropole would not have been extravagant enough to get the tabloids' attention.

"The moment your spade dipped into the crap everything changed forever. I'll get such big bucks from your photos that I'm not charging you."

"Naturally, you can stay here overnight," Edna continued where Papparazzi had ended.

Ismo was grateful and moved over the expression of goodwill. Edna topped off their glasses and suggested that before retiring they could make proposals on the headlines following the comedian's sneak attack. Their creativity was literally bursting: Shit flew on the Soho Club, Viewers caught in the rain of poo, Faeces strike in Covent Garden, Comedian soiled his audience with horseshit, *The God's Theatre* stank in London and Come and do my laundry, pig!

That's how the billboards and sensational headlines were like in real life anyway.

MIND THE GAP!

The escalator of Leicester Square underground station appeared to be very, very long as Edna and Papparazzi descended down to the platform area. The bright eyes had literally caught Pappy with his pants down, when she had lured him to join her to a no-pants underground tour, which was arranged yearly in January. The escapade toughened its participants and broke the winter's back. Since the brunette had guessed her better half had not-so-presentable underwear on, she had brought him a pair of brand-new Finland underpants, which he had pulled on top of his undeniably shabby briefs.

"You look the best wearing blue and white," Edna stated the fact.

The ultimate female had stripy hotpants on. Her upper body was covered with a lightweight jacket, Papparazzi had a windcheater. The Finn had stashed his coat and both of their pants into his back bag. Obeying Edna's request, he hadn't taken his camera bag with him. This was a day of fun and games, no work involved. They were surrounded with a similar fun-loving crowd. After Edna had familiarised herself with the Finnish lunacy like throwing shit among the audience, she wanted to introduce to her beloved the aspects of London's nutty madness.

"It's something we can accomplish as well as you Northern Vikings, believe it or not!"

Although Papparazzi was not the shyest of men, he felt the gazes of fully-dressed passengers prickling his skin. He felt awkward. If being still single, he by no means would have put himself into a mess like this. Although they were deep under the ground, the chills dug into his bones down to the nuclei. Fortunately, Edna had brought a hip flask to keep them warm and also to lift their spirits up. They stepped into a Northern Line train following on the heels of the group leader who held a green umbrella up in the air.

"Imagine all the people going naked under and above the ground," Edna whispered to her sweetie pie's ear.

The pure thought of it made Papparazzi chuckle. It was made clear that clothes made a civilised person. Without them the whole shebang turned into a comedy. Edna started to giggle as well. Very soon they reached their destination at Waterloo Station where a bunch of underwear travellers had gathered up to have a party. They all shouted "Mind the gap!" at the time of taking a group photo just to relax the atmosphere. Immediately thereafter, they joined forces to do dance moves. The hands whisking in the same rhythm to the right and left; heads following the movement. The show was finished with cabaret hands. Papparazzi was also letting go from the bottom of his heart under the bright lights: trepak, spectacular jumps and slips followed one another as solo acts. He also piggybacked his sweetheart. They were rewarded with applauses.

Since the original rag gang had scattered into pieces in Waterloo, they took the return trip just by themselves contemplating the ultimate intention behind the no-pants underground travel.

"There are hundreds of reasons you can choose whichever pleases you the most. One of them is to punch holes in the glass walls separating people," Edna suspected.

"In that case this going around with bare legs corresponds

with sauna in my homeland. When you go there, you have no titles."

Edna and Papparazzi's conversation came to a halt because they saw something unexpected. At Charing Cross station George Bamby emerged at the other end of the carriage in his blue-red-and-white suit. He must have received a hot tip and very specific coordinates of Edna and Papparazzi going around naked or at any case almost naked. The train took off with speed. Bamby began to capture the two of them hanging on the pole with his camera. They had no place to hide due to the heavy crowd. The Union Jack guy really hit the jackpot this time! That was the only thought in Papparazzi's head. He, if anyone, knew how important a role luck was playing in getting the top shot. When he had collected enough frames, near and far, the paparazzo introduced the lovey doves to the fellow passengers with the challenge he had thrown in to his colleague, once he had entered the shores of the foggy island.

"Victory is mine! I scored a hat trick!"

The crowd cheered wildly. Papparazzi and Edna tried to save their skin by pointing out the missing sensation on the shooting session. They were only harmless and pantsless underground passengers among hundreds of other Londoners.

"Do you really think you can make any money out of these shots at all?"

The answer was floated with confidence.

"I will certainly get a fair amount of money out of them. Last time when you two were in front of my lens, neither of you had any clothes on. Now you are wearing some. That's a sensation isn't it!"

SHOP 'TIL YOU DROP

Papparazzi was spending his tranquil Sunday in Café Concerto in Knightsbridge. He had been in Hyde Park in order to take photos of water birds and rowers on the Serpentine for his own pleasure, now it was time to reward himself with a cup of coffee and scones. His zen-like serenity got shattered, as he saw a sudden crowd gathering on the other side of the Brompton Road. Probably Harrods was starting a discount campaign of some sort. He asked a waiter to join him in order to inquire what the commotion was all about. The waiter assumed they were expecting a visit of some celebrity loaded with money or maybe one of the Arab Sheiks ready to spend their cash in the emporium. He hit the waiter with a tenner without waiting for the change and rushed out with his camera bag.

    The mob was blocking the road congesting the car traffic. Angry honking echoed and fingers were given. The shooter squeezed himself in the back of the pack in order to take a good look at which of the filthy rich celebs were being brought in on the black limos and cabs. The visibility was really poor. He heard somebody in the crowd exclaiming: "The Royalties! Our very own Royalties!" Hearing this, Papparazzi got strong as a bear as he bulldozed himself with his elbows towards the crown heads. There was no way he could get into the front row seat but near enough to the black cars to get pictures on the event. Once Queen Elizabeth the Second appeared on the scene, the sea of people roared so enthusiastically, making one want to put the earplugs on. The Queen walked slowly towards the green-coated doorman. Miraculously the photographer was able to dig out his camera and get the target on the highest member of the kingdom. Click, click! More dignifiedly dressed welcomers on behalf of the emporium emerged on the doorway guiding the majesty inside. The noise risen by Prince William and his spouse Catherine was so loud that one would have needed noise-cancelling headphones to subdue it. William was wearing a red and black ceremonial uniform with blue shoulder straps and gold braids and Kate had a blue dress accompanied by a bolero of the same fabric. Papparazzi steamed on so fast he felt his forefinger almost cramping. He was also able to capture a photo of Prince Harry although line-cutters and jostlers were everywhere. Fortunately, Meghan wasn't at his side; the couple was so popular that the noise would have been supersonic. The first goers into the store were followed by a number of shoppers in their well-fitted clothes. But that's not all! On the side of the store began as a group song, 'God Save The Queen'. This was the strongest sign of patriotism Papparazzi had ever been offered by the Brits so far. There was also a spicy afterthought of the crown heads putting their Visas on the grinder in the sums exceeding seven figures.

Due to the shooters gathering there in flocks, Papparazzi knew his would be the more expensive ones the sooner he got them into *London Star*. He dashed to his car in order to hustle. The visions of the big bucks flashed through his mind too. The fall from the heights was harsh and grim. Graham thanked him in his answering email of his contribution stating they had no use of the footage in the newspaper. "I'm sorry, Pappy! It seems to me that you haven't been in London long enough to have pumped into your colleague Alison Jackson's works of art and performances. Her speciality is the doppelgangers of the celebrities adventuring anytime anywhere. This time she and the royalty doubles are having a PR-event in Harrods. We were notified well ahead in advance but it didn't go over our publication threshold. Since you made a such an effort on a holy day like this, we might be able to squeeze one or two of them in the corner of one page. Unfortunately, we can only manage to pay a pittance for these kind of fillers. You have no idea how sorry I am for all of this."

These were those fucked up moments when nitro-popping people lost their lives. Not Papparazzi by all means. After taking a moment to recover from the blow he went on with his messaging: "Why on earth was everyone so excited knowing they were just copies of the gentry?"

The answer came aptly: "The cheerers were well aware what was going on but it didn't slow down their excitement. The truth is that the celebs cannot be lured into all kinds of openings of an envelope so people book their doubles to come. The imitation passes as the real thing. That's us Brits for you. You Finns have no understanding of these matters at all."

The camera hero was stunned. If he had been dealing with the comic book *Asterix the Gaul* instead of *London Star*, there would have been a bubble above his head with a text: "These Englishmen are barmy!"

AURORA BOREALIS WITH LOVE

Papparazzi and Edna had travelled to the Finnish Lapland. The lovebirds were residing in the Kakslauttanen Arctic Resort Hotel, which was situated in the Northern side of the Arctic Circle. They were lying down on an opulent king-sized inside of a glass-roofed igloo looking at the night sky. The weather outside was so cold it could even freeze a yoik; inside it was warm enough to make them take off their clothes. The dark black painting had been painted by a heavenly lichen bearded with his paint brush. Green, red and white arms of flames intertwined with each other in the heights moving swiftly and capriciously like a Siberian jay. Radiant, constantly mutating arches filled the skyline, as if the colours were running down on a dark-coloured canvas. The celestial lights played on them making the rosy lady's hair look like golden grass spotted with wild rosemary flowers.

Once they had seen enough of the Fire fox's tail-whipping, they turned the lights off in the bedroom and dug out the laptop. Edna was anxious to see more of the colourful pictures of Lapland. They supported themselves with pillows in a comfy sitting position. Papparazzi tapped artist Reidar Särestöniemi's world of colours on to the screen. The images rolled on in the rhythm of a slide show until they stopped to have a more in-depth look at the creation called the Evening Red. The landscape was dominated by red. As they viewed it longer, the blurred visions of humans and animals began to appear in front of their eyes alongside shrubs and shallow bushes. Shades of yellow, green and brown made an impression of the stony and tree-stumped ground. The layering of the paint surfaces invigorated the scene.

"Just as you think you know what you are seeing, new and surprising elements are popping out," Edna described.

The yellow and red melted into each other ardently in the ringing colours of spring. A peculiar memory of the artist splashed into Papparazzi's mind.

"Once Reidar started to get proper compensation for his creations, he searched liberation of the bondage of mammon by burning notes in the sauna furnace."

"If this had been an *Asterix* cartoon, there would be a bubble written on it: those Finns are barmy!" Edna cracked.

The igloo vibrated with laughter making the laptop fall on the blanket bend. He sensed this would be the right time for the surprise he had fostered like a reindeer mother of its calf for the whole journey. He climbed out of the bed with a secretive face to the wardrobe, returning with something in his hand and asked Edna to stand up beside the bed as well. Once she did what was asked, Papparazzi picked up a bronze necklace.

"What have you got there?" she asked.

"*The Heart of Utajärvi*," he whispered as he slipped it fondly around the beauty's neck.

It was the birth place of Papparazzi. The necklace was the biggest sign of love a son of Oulu river valley could give to his girl. The swirls inside it formed a butterfly. The star-eyed-one who had her heart in the right place was the only rightful recipient of the pendant. Edna filled that condition with the clarity of the ice.

"Does this mean proposal?"

He nodded, adding they could get the proper engagement rings once they got back to London.

A slight smile crept onto Edna's face as her eyes were filled with tears of joy. The gaze of a woman in love took their time in burning Papparazzi until the excitement erupted to an affirmative and passionate embrace.

A CHIRRUP TO PIMLICO

Papparazzi and Edna were having coffee in the back of the Pimlico Village. The backdoor of the tiny café leading into a small courtyard decorated with green plants was open. In the background the sound of the hit singer Doris Day's evergreen song 'Que Sera, Sera' fitted the ambiance. As we didn't know of the future, we should leave it to fate. Maybe so. The decoration of the café with its blue and white colours was well fitted to the Finn's taste. Both of the coffee drinkers wore glimmering golden rings. Edna's gaze was glued into a painting where a living model was posing in a drawing class. The naked model was painted nude – leaving the rest of the picture monochrome. The creation breathed 1920s. Papparazzi was browsing a picture of the historical past of Warwick Street. It was no wonder the art work caught their eyes since they were just returning from Tate Britain. They had agreed that John Singer Sargent's *Carnation, Lily, Lily, Rose* and John William Waterhouse's *The Lady of Shalott* had been the most memorable works in the Museum of Arts. They had also seen landscape artist J.M.W. Turner's collection but only cursorily.

"It became clear to me in our visit that an artist must have full freedom in creating their own things. The street art in the Pimlico underground station is like that. It wakes us up in our everyday life to sense and think more. It kicks in the balls!" Papparazzi ranted.

In the middle of the conversation, they drank good coffee

and felt the health effects of the delicious cupcakes starting to kick off. The tension between the two of them started to rise, as they were getting closer to the moment of truth. They had watched the film *Eat, Pray, Love* on the previous night. The parts where the characters were asked to describe themselves with only one word had struck Edna's chord.

"The one well-thought word characterized them better than the thousands of words pouring out from their mouths."

"Tell me about it!"

One word from *Eat, Pray, Love* stood out over the others: attraversiamo, to cross over.

"Attraversiamo is Italian. Fortunately it wasn't the Portuguese saudade, because the author Elizabeth Gilbert would have been forced to double the pages of her novel in order to define it. Portuguese poets and other scribblers are inventing new definitions to it every day."

"If you had your back against the wall in order to determine that in one word what would it be?"

"Yearning,"

The two of them had made a plea to tell their own words on the spot there and then. Edna got there first to utter her question.

"What is your word, my beloved one?"

Papparazzi took a significant break before making his important revelation.

"Passion."

"That's hitting the mark! We also agreed to give reasons to the chosen word. What is yours?"

"I'm passionate in everything I do."

"Accepted."

The tension intensified further. Edna was well aware of the worth of holding the other party in her claws for a bit more.

Finally, Papparazzi let his curiosity on the loose:

"Well, which word is the best in describing you?"

"I must confess that I had to handle this matter more thoroughly than I ever imagined, but I got the right one at the crack of dawn: noble-minded."

"It defines you perfectly but why that is word among all of the words in the world the one?"

"Because I'm letting you be passionate!"

Bright laughter filled the café including the employee. Sheena couldn't have helped herself but listen to the last part of the conversation. She offered them free refills of mocha rewarding them for the sweetest laughs of the day. Once they had finished, another kind of thirst kept on growing. A bottle of wine was waiting for them in the fridge of Papparazzi's lodgings. In *Eat, Pray, Love* it was called the therapist. As the Passion and the Noble-Minded were exiting the facilities, the smell of the fumes and the spring flowers on Lupus Street flooded on their faces. They walked arm in arm on the pavement chit-chatting and hugging each other once in a while. They passed a small park, which was beside the building where the snowbird Papparazzi had found his nest. Rays of sunlight glinted romantically, when they crossed the street at Pimlico Primary School playgrounds. The white residence with its blue door greeted them. The rise on the stairs was cut with kisses on the landing. Once the lovebirds reached the loft apartment, they saw how the natural light landed from the windows into their nest creating silhouettes and shadows, illuminating the sensitive moment. After taking off their outerwear, the engaged couple enjoyed liquid therapy from their glasses and cuddled on the sofa-bed listening to sweet tunes inspired by the sounds of the Pimlico Village café. Especially the singer Kristiina Halkola's interpretation of the evergreen 'Not a

Half' which made the Passion and Noble-Minded get goose bumps:

"No, I don't need a half,
Give me a whole heaven and earth,
Oceans and rivers and the mountain ridges,
Mine, I'm not going to share.
No, you life won't caress me with a half,
Everything as a whole, I can take it,
I don't want half of happiness,
And neither I want half of sorrow
I just want the half of the pillow,
Which tenderly against your cheek,
As a helpless star, as a falling star,
A ring glides in your finger…"